ROB CHILDS

THE BIG

CUP COLLECTION

including
THE BIG CLASH
THE BIG DROP
THE BIG SEND-OFF

THE BIG CUP COLLECTION
A YOUNG CORGI BOOK : 9780552547642

Published in Great Britain in 2003 by Corgi Books,
an imprint of Random House Children's Books

Young Corgi Books are published by Random House Children's Books,
61–63 Uxbridge Road, London W5 5SA,
A Random House Group Company

Addresses for companies within The Random House Group Limited
can be found at: www.randomhouse.co.uk/offices.htm

THE RANDOM HOUSE GROUP Limited Reg. No. 954009

www.**kids**at**random**house.co.uk

The Random House Group Limited supports The Forest Stewardship
Council (FSC), the leading international forest certification organisation.
All our titles that are printed on Greenpeace approved FSC certified paper
carry the FSC logo. Our paper procurement policy can be found at:
www.rbooks.co.uk/environment.

Mixed Sources
Product group from well-managed
forests and other controlled sources
www.fsc.org Cert no. TT-COC-2139
FSC © 1996 Forest Stewardship Council

A CIP catalogue record for this book is available from the British Library.

Printed and bound in Great Britain by
Cox & Wyman Ltd, Reading, Berkshire

THE BIG FOOTBALL COLLECTION
*includes The Big Game, The Big Match and
The Big Prize*

THE BIG FOOTBALL TREBLE
*includes The Big Chance, The Big Break and
The Big Star*

THE BIG FOOTBALL FRENZY
*includes The Big Fix, The Big Freeze and
The Big Win*

Published by Corgi Pups Books,
for beginner readers:

GREAT SAVE!
GREAT SHOT!
GREAT HIT!
GREAT GOAL!
WICKED CATCH!
WICKED DAY!

ROB CHILDS
THE BIG CLASH

Illustrated by Aidan Potts

Especially for all goalkeepers —my own favourite position.

1 On the Way

The ball bobbled crazily about the goalmouth.

'What a scramble!'

'It's in this time – must be.'

'No! Another corner. Keeper's saved it again.'

'He's having a blinder.'

'We should be six up by now.'

The home supporters could hardly believe that their team still hadn't managed to score. Hanfield Juniors had been on top for so much of the match, but the cup quarter-final remained deadlocked at 0-0.

The corner-kick landed safely in the arms of Chris Weston, Danebridge's goalkeeper and captain, and he clutched the ball to his jersey.

'That ball's like a boomerang,' laughed Philip, their lanky central defender. 'It keeps on coming back to you.'

'Just one of those days, I guess,' Chris said with a grin. He felt in great form and was enjoying himself tremendously.

He had even saved a penalty before half-time, diving the right way to turn the kick around the post. His side were now only a few minutes away from earning a replay, but Hanfield refused to give up.

No sooner had Chris booted the ball upfield than it was back once more in his own penalty area. Philip tried to scoop it clear, but the ball fell to an attacker who chested it down and caught it sweetly on the volley.

'Goa—!' yelled one of the parents on the touchline.

The cry was choked off. There was a flash of green across the goal and in the next instant the ball changed course and flipped over the crossbar.

'Ohh! Fantastic save! That kid's unbeatable.'

Chris's grandad led the applause and turned to Danebridge's head-master.

'How much longer to hold out?' he asked anxiously.

Mr Jones glanced at his watch. 'A couple of minutes, that's all,' he said and then shouted a warning to his team. 'Mark up tight, reds.'

They need not have worried. Chris leapt high to claim the ball from the corner, knowing that Hanfield had committed themselves fully to the attack. They'd left only two defenders back to cope with any breakaway.

The captain also knew that Danebridge had the ideal pair of

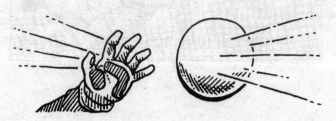

strikers to take advantage of that situation. They were both fast with good dribbling skills. One was Rakesh Patel, their leading scorer, and the other had proved equally deadly in front of goal since coming into the team after Christmas. She was Kerry Sharpe, the first girl to wear the red and white stripes of Danebridge.

Chris's long kick sailed wide to Rakesh on his right. The winger flicked the ball further ahead and gave chase, and there was no way that the chubby full-back could catch him. Meanwhile Kerry darted to the left to try and drag the other opponent away and create more space for Rakesh.

Hanfield's last defender had a problem. Should he go and challenge the winger or stay with the girl?

Forced to make a choice, he decided Rakesh was the main danger and moved over to block his route to goal.

Rakesh had to choose what to do now. He fancied taking the boy on himself, but Kerry was unmarked and screaming for the ball. If he messed up the chance, he was certain to get a mouthful from her about being greedy. He played safe. Kerry Sharpe had a tongue to match her name!

Rakesh timed his pass to perfection, slipping the ball inside as the defender lunged in to tackle. With the keeper drawn out of position to cover a possible shot from the winger, Kerry had the goal at her mercy.

She didn't bother to control the ball. She just hit it first time as it rolled across her path. It was a clean

strike, but for one awful split-second, Kerry thought it was going to miss the target. The ball veered to one side and snicked the post as it sped into the net.

The late goal came as a cruel blow for Hanfield. As Kerry celebrated with her dancing teammates, the home side stared at one another in shock that Danebridge had grabbed the vital winner. They barely had time to kick off again before the referee blew his whistle for the end of the game.

Chris felt slightly embarrassed as he shook hands with the opposing captain. 'Well played, you didn't deserve to lose today,' he said.

'Dead right, there,' the boy muttered. 'Without you, Danebridge would have been massacred.'

The players gathered around Mr

Jones briefly before heading for home. 'One shot, one goal, that's all it takes sometimes to win a match,' he told them. 'Teams often need a bit of luck in the cup.'

'When's the Final, Mr Jones?' asked Kerry.

'Whoa! Hold your horses,' he chuckled, especially for the benefit of pony-mad Kerry. 'One fence at a time, young lady. We've still got the semi-final to come yet.'

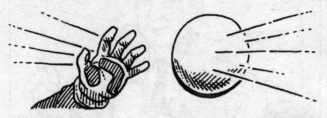

'Yes, I know,' she replied. 'But I'd like to get a medal.'

'Let's hope you will. No reason why not.'

Kerry was about to drop a bombshell on her team's chances of cup glory. 'Well, there is, you see. If the Final's not till after the holidays, it'll be too late,' she explained. 'I'm leaving at Easter!'

2 *Out of the Blue*

'It's a shame you'll be losing Kerry,' said Grandad on Sunday afternoon.

Chris was gazing through Grandad's kitchen window at the group of lads kicking a ball about on the recreation ground. They were his brother Andrew's mates who had all left primary school the year before.

He nodded in agreement. 'She's the same age as me. We were expecting she'd still be here to play for us next season as well.'

'Didn't anybody know she was leaving?'

'Kerry only found out herself a few days ago. Her parents have just bought a riding school and stables in another county.'

There was a rap on the back door and Andrew burst in – but not as fast as the panting bundle of fur that brushed past his legs.

'Saw Shoot in the garden, so I guessed you'd be here, our kid,' said Andrew as their black and white collie scampered up to Grandad for some fuss. 'Fancy a game of footie with the gang? We need another keeper.'

'Sorry, Mum's sent me out to give him a walk.'

'Who – Grandad or the dog?'

'Cheeky monkey,' Grandad laughed. 'You're right, mind, I could do with a spot of exercise. Go on, off with you both. I'll walk Shoot.'

Grandad followed the brothers out and leant against the garden wall of his cottage to watch them play for a while. Shoot had other ideas. He nosed at his lead that was draped over the wall and looked up, whining.

'OK, OK, I get the message,' chuckled Grandad. 'You win.'

As Grandad set off and threw a stick for the dog to chase, he kept an eye on the footballers. He saw Chris dive low to his left to smother a shot from Tim Lawrence, last year's school team captain.

'Good stop, Chris,' Tim called out. 'I heard about your great display yesterday. Hope you go on to win the cup.'

'Yeah, they might do the double – win the cup and get relegated!' scoffed Andrew. 'League position's a bit dodgy, little brother.'

Chris pulled a face at him. 'We'll stay up, don't worry.'

'Thanks to a girl, maybe,' Andrew chortled. 'You'll have to make sure you play all your games before she goes.'

'We've got Rakesh too – and others. We're not a one-man team.'

'One-girl team you mean!'

Grandad wandered along the bank of the narrow River Dane, amused at Shoot's antics in the water. It wasn't so funny, though, when the dog returned with the stick and shook his fur dry right next to him.

Grandad turned away to protect himself, just in time to see Chris pull off another fine reflex save. 'That's m'boy,' Grandad murmured proudly.

'He's got goalie's blood in his veins, all right. No doubt about that.'

Chris had always wanted to be a goalie. Just like his grandad. Or even perhaps like his dad who used to play in goal for the village team too. Not any more. Tony Weston had left home over three years ago and disappeared abroad. They hadn't seen him since.

Danebridge were back in league action in the first week of March, a home game after school on Wednesday versus local rivals Shenby.

The two schools were always keen to do well against each other, but there was an extra edge to this

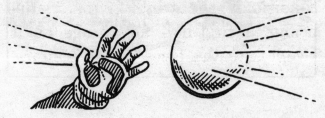

match. Shenby were pushing for the league title, while Danebridge were peering anxiously over their shoulders at the relegation zone.

'One thing's for sure,' Mr Jones told the players at their team meeting at morning break. 'If you let Shenby have as many chances as Hanfield, they'll punish you. Don't expect them to be so wasteful.'

'Chris will gobble up anything that gets past us,' Philip grinned, nudging the captain playfully on the arm. 'He's red-hot at the minute.'

'A good job too,' said the headmaster. 'Though I'm sure he'd like to see the other keeper having his hands warmed up as well.'

The match kicked off in blustery conditions, the wind giving Dane-bridge a first-half advantage as it swept into the faces of the visitors.

Grandad watched from his garden as usual, well muffled in coat, scarf, gloves and cap. Shoot was also there but had no interest in the football. He was eyeing a cat that sat warily on the wall nearby.

Shenby started the stronger, playing neat football into the wind by keeping their passes short and accurate. They seemed much quicker to the ball than Danebridge and Chris was kept busy, grateful to see a snapshot skim wide of the far post.

'C'mon! Get stuck in,' he urged his team. 'They're all over us.'

Philip tried to find Rakesh on the wing with a long, diagonal pass, but not even the swift Rakesh could catch the wind-assisted ball as it ran out of play. The ball was kicked back for a Shenby throw-in by Andrew who had just arrived, still in the

uniform of Selworth Comprehensive.

Shoot began to bark, but it wasn't the usual joyous greeting. It was a warning aimed at the stranger who was with his young master. It alerted Grandad and he held on to the lead more tightly.

If Shoot was alarmed, Grandad was even more so when he looked at the man properly and saw who it was. His son-in-law!

'Hello again, Pop. Long time no see. How are you?'

Tony Weston didn't wait for an answer, nodding towards the Danebridge goalkeeper. 'Nice to see young Chris keeping up the family tradition, eh? Andy tells me Chris is captain too. He must be good.'

'He is,' Grandad stated firmly. 'He'll be better than you or me ever were.'

At that moment, the Shenby number nine was put clean through down the middle with only the goalkeeper to beat.

'Out, Chris, out!' came the loud shout. 'Narrow the angle.'

Chris was distracted by the oddly familiar voice and glanced towards the cottage. He was so shocked, he barely made a move to stop the striker dribbling round him and slotting the ball into the back of the net.

'Why didn't you dive at his feet?' the man yelled as Chris still stared his way. 'You just let him waltz past you.'

Andrew noticed the look of dismay on Grandad's face. 'Er, I think you might have put Chris off a bit there, Dad.'

3 Shoot First...

'What's the matter, Chris?' asked Mr Jones at half-time. 'Are you feeling all right?'

Chris nodded weakly, but his face was as pale as a blank sheet of paper. He kept looking in bewilderment towards the row of cottages and the headmaster followed his gaze, recognizing Mr Weston. 'I didn't know *he* was back on the scene,' he said to himself. 'No wonder the boy's upset.'

Danebridge were now 2-0 down and Chris felt guilty about both goals. The second had trickled between his legs as he took his eye off the ball at the last moment, rattled by another ill-timed bellow from his dad.

As he took up his position in goal for the second half, Dad called to him again. 'C'mon, Chris, wake up! Show them what you're made of.'

'You can't shout out like that at Chris,' Grandad protested to his son-in-law. 'You know he takes things to heart.'

Dad sighed heavily. 'I always did seem to hurt his feelings too easily. Never meant to, I just speak before I think. He'll have to learn that my bark's worse than my bite.'

'Shoot's good at both,' grinned Andrew and then a thought struck him. 'Does Mum know you're here?'

'No, not yet. Might be best for you to tell her first, eh? I don't reckon she'd want me suddenly turning up on the doorstep!'

'You could have warned us all that you were coming,' Grandad remarked. 'How long are you planning on staying?'

'Trying to get rid of me already, are you, Pop?' he grinned, then

answered more seriously. 'Not sure. I need to sort a few things out.'

'Dad picked me up from school in this dead flash car,' Andrew boasted.

'Only hired,' his dad put in. 'But I've got three over in Spain.'

'Three cars! Wow! Are you rich?'

He laughed. 'No, but I'm working on it. Spain's a wonderful country. You'd love it, Andy. Hot sunshine, beaches – great football teams . . .'

'Hold on,' said Grandad. 'Don't go filling his head with all that sort of crazy stuff. He doesn't realize you're joking.'

'No joke, Pop. He's still my son. What's wrong with the idea that he might want to come and live with me instead?'

Shoot picked up the tension between the two men and began to growl again, eyes fixed on the stranger.

'Quiet, Shoot,' ordered Andrew. 'Sorry, Dad. It's just that he doesn't know you yet. Mum bought him for us after you left.'

'She's obviously got him well trained. I don't reckon he likes me.'

'He's got good judgement,' said Grandad stiffly, turning his attention back to the match.

Danebridge were finding it difficult even to get the ball into Shenby's half of the pitch. The combined power of the wind and Shenby's attacks forced them to defend deep, battling away in the hope of keeping the score down. Rakesh and Kerry up front were almost like spectators.

Chris became aware of his dad wandering down the touchline and he tried in vain to keep focused on the game. Dad was soon right behind his goal.

'Hiya, son. How about pulling off a great save for your old dad, eh?'

Chris ignored him, not even turning round.

'C'mon, don't be like that. Haven't seen you for ages.'

'Nearly four years.' Chris was unable to resist pointing that out.

'I send you birthday cards.'

'They're always late. What are you doing back here, anyway?'

'I've come to find out how you're all getting on. Andy was pleased to see me again. And I was hoping you would be too.'

Chris didn't answer. A long, raking pass had split the defence wide open. The ball reached the unmarked left-winger, who had time and space to steady himself and set his sights for a shot at goal.

The ball fizzed to Chris's right, aimed for the gap between him and the post, and he flung himself down low to parry it. The winger was quick to recover and tried to head the rebound over the grounded goalie, but Chris's reactions were just as

sharp. He sprang up and clawed the ball out of the air to turn it aside for a corner. It was a spectacular double save.

'Magic!' Dad praised him. 'I'd have been proud of that in my day.'

Mr Jones held up play. 'I'm sorry, Mr Weston, please don't stand there. Your son needs to have his full concentration on the game.'

'Didn't do too badly just then, did he?' he replied sarcastically.

'Even so,' the headmaster insisted, trying to be polite. 'Please…'

'OK, OK, I'm going. I know when I'm not welcome,' he scowled. 'We'll talk another time, Chris, eh? Get to know each other better.'

He slouched away towards the car park, intending to find a hotel in Selworth. He wasn't expecting an invitation to stay in Grandad's cottage.

Chris felt all churned up inside. Half of him wanted nothing more to do with his dad. The other half wanted to call him back. He caught the headmaster's eye and gave a little helpless shrug.

Mr Jones breathed a sigh and blew his whistle. 'Play on, lads. Play on.'

'How well do you remember Dad?'

Andrew's voice cut through the darkness of the bedroom he shared with his brother. They'd spent all evening discussing their father with Mum, but it hadn't been easy. She still felt bitter about the way that he had deserted them.

'Not as well as you do, it seems,' Chris replied, 'judging by how pally you two were this afternoon, according to Grandad.'

'Well, I'm older than you. You were

only about six when he left, still in
the Infants. I was eight. That makes
a difference.'

'We're different too. Mum always
says I take more after Grandad and
that you're more like Dad – but without his good looks!'

Andrew chuckled. 'Can't help it.
It's just the way I am, I guess. Shoot
first, ask questions later, that's me –
even on the soccer pitch!'

'I've noticed. What was Dad like himself in goal, d'you know?'

'Dead loud! He could have shouted for England. You could hear him a mile off yelling things at his team.'

'He hasn't changed much then,' Chris muttered.

'Give him a chance, little brother. He's OK really – just gets a bit carried away at times. We used to have loads of fun together. Remember him playing footie with us in the garden and on the recky?'

'Vaguely. But Dad coming back like this is bound to cause some trouble. He's made me make a mess of things already today.'

'Yeah, what was it in the end, four-nil? You lot were so bad, I reckon you were lucky to get nil! Think you'll avoid getting relegated?'

'Still got three games left. We'll do it,'

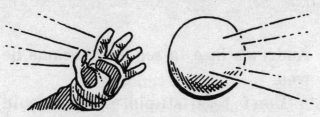

Chris said, crossing his fingers under the duvet. 'Kerry's around till Easter.'

Andrew was silent for a minute before he spoke again, somewhat hesitantly. 'Um . . . Kerry might not be the only one on the move. . .'

'How d'you mean?' said Chris, worried about further losses for his team. 'Who else is leaving?'

'Me – maybe.'

'*You!* What are you going on about?'

'Well, I've been thinking about a few things Dad said. Y'know, about Spain. Sounds like a fantastic place to live . . .'

His voice trailed away, testing his brother's reaction. Chris sat bolt upright in bed, trying to make out

Andrew's face to see how serious he was.

'Don't talk stupid. Mum would never let you go off abroad with Dad.'

'How could she stop me?'

Chris was flummoxed for a moment. 'I don't know, but I'm sure she could. There must be some kind of law against it. Like kidnapping.'

'*Kidnapping!*' Andrew snorted. 'Now who's talking stupid? How can you be kidnapped by your own dad?'

Chris scratched his head. He still thought it wasn't allowed. 'Has Dad actually asked you to go back with him?'

'Not as such,' Andrew admitted.

'No, I bet he doesn't really want to have you cluttering the place up. Besides, you'd miss going on that special coaching course at Easter.'

'Yeah, realized that myself. It

could be my big break, if the coaches there like the look of me.'

'Be an even bigger break here if you did go to Spain,' Chris murmured. 'It'd split the family in two.'

That was the end of their conversation. They didn't even bother to say good night to each other.

4 Family Affairs

The school team squad were back on the recky the following afternoon for their usual Thursday practice session. It was a good chance for them to run the Shenby defeat out of their system.

'Which is more important, d'yer reckon, the league or the cup?' Philip said as he and Chris sat on the grass, tying up their bootlaces before the start. 'I mean, if you had to choose.'

'Both!' answered Chris. 'We still

need a few more league points to be safe, but we also want to win the semi-final next week.'

A football suddenly whistled over their heads and smacked into the wall of the wooden changing hut, making them jump.

'Sorry, guys,' Rakesh laughed. 'I was aiming at you.'

'That's why we're near the bottom of the league,' Philip muttered. 'Our so-called leading scorer can't even hit a couple of sitting ducks!'

After a vigorous warm-up, Mr Jones organized the players into small groups for some much-needed shooting practice. 'You don't have to leave all the scoring up to Rakesh and Kerry, you know,' he told them. 'If you fancy a go at goal, then have a crack. Don't be afraid of missing.'

Chris showed no fear at all when he tried his luck with a few shots as well. He only managed to get one of them on target between the cones.

'Best stick to what you're good at,' grinned Philip.

'Right, I am better at stopping shots,' said Chris. 'Usually.'

'Forget about what happened yesterday. We all have our bad games.'

When Chris returned to goal, he enjoyed his little duel with Rakesh. Out of five efforts, Rakesh only succeeded in beating Chris once. Neither would have admitted it, but they were both counting.

So was Ryan. The youngster was only in Year 4 and he was delighted to put the ball past the captain twice. He'd already scored for the school team as a substitute and the headmaster decided it was about time to name him in the starting line-up.

In the practice match that

followed, Ryan's excellent goal clinched his selection for the semi-final. Kerry was demanding a pass but he had the confidence to go it alone, despite the narrow angle. His shot was as straight as a laser beam, the ball skidding under Chris's dive and scraping the cone on its way in.

'Great strike!' praised Mr Jones before Kerry could moan at Ryan for

not passing. 'If you don't shoot, you don't score – that's what they say in football. And goals are what the game is all about!'

Andrew arrived home later than Chris that evening, enthusing about his own performance in a league match for Selworth's Year 7 side.

'Won six-one!' he bragged to Chris, disturbing his attempts at doing some homework at their bedroom desk. 'Tim got a couple and the poor guy I was marking never had a kick. Apart from a few on his legs, that is!'

'How come they managed to score if you were so brilliant in defence?' muttered Chris as he wrestled with a tricky maths problem.

'Not my fault. Our goalie played a bit like you – useless!'

Chris ignored the taunt, knowing it was just his brother's way of trying to get his attention. Andrew wasn't one to give up easily.

'Dad came to watch me,' he went on. 'Shouted out quite a lot, like he does, but the ref deserved it. Talk about biased. He disallowed about three more of our goals.'

Andrew was becoming frustrated at the lack of response as Mum called them downstairs for tea.

'Don't tell Mum, but I'm full already,' he said, affecting a burp. 'Dad took me and Tim for a Giant Superburger in Selworth.'

'Bribes now, is it?'

'What d'yer mean by that?'

'Nothing,' Chris said innocently. 'Has he bought you a bullfighting outfit as well?'

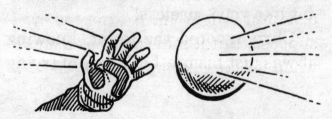

'Ah, right. I see what you're getting at now,' Andrew sneered. 'No, he hasn't – or a Real Madrid strip either, before you ask.'

Chris stood up from the desk. 'So have you made up your mind about going to sunny Spain?'

His brother gave a shrug. 'Plenty of time. We haven't discussed it yet. Dad's not leaving till he's finished his business here.'

'And what business *is* that exactly?'

Andrew was suddenly serious, dropping his act of bravado. 'It's to do with Mum. She met Dad in town today to talk things over. They've decided to get a divorce.'

'Oh . . .' Chris sat down again with a bump. 'Might have expected it, I suppose. But it still comes as a shock when it actually happens.'

'Come on, boys,' Mum called up once more. 'Your tea's ready. I'm not prepared to wait for ever, you know.'

Danebridge School was gripped by cup fever. They'd been drawn at home in the semi-final against Great Norton.

'If we're on form, we ought to beat them,' said Rakesh as he stuck another poster on the wall outside his classroom. It advertised the big match and appealed for supporters to cheer on the team.

'At least we've avoided Shenby,' Philip piped up, doing the same job further down the corridor. 'They must be the cup favourites.'

Chris admired his pals' artistic efforts. He'd pinned his own on the side of the recky changing hut. 'We'll save Shenby for the Final, with a bit

of luck,' he said. 'We've got a score to settle with them!'

'Yeah, a four-nil one,' Rakesh cackled.

One person who intended to be at the semi-final was Chris's mum.

'The shopping can wait next Saturday,' she told him one teatime. 'If your dad's going to watch the match, like he says, then so shall I.'

'You never went to see me play for Danebridge,' Andrew said sourly.

'I'm not very interested in football, as you well know,' Mum said with a frown. 'You two get all that from Grandad – and your father, of course.'

Chris took Shoot out later for an evening walk around the village to mull things over. He found himself,

almost automatically, at Grandad's cottage. Grandad poured him a cold drink and filled Shoot's bowl with fresh water.

'What's on your mind, m'boy? Problem parents?'

Chris nodded. 'You never know what they'll do next. Both Mum and Dad are going to be at the game. That'll be really weird.'

'Don't worry,' Grandad chuckled. 'I'll be there too, as always. I'll make sure there's no crowd trouble!'

It was said partly in jest, but Grandad knew that football matches tended to bring out the very worst in his impulsive son-in-law. He was expecting fireworks – the kind that suddenly go off bang!

5 Crowd Trouble

'C'mon, ref! That was a corner. Came off a defender.'

The semi-final had only been underway for five minutes when Tony Weston let rip for the first time. He was standing near the halfway line with Andrew, a few metres away from Grandad, Mum and Shoot.

The neutral referee was pointing for a goal-kick to Great Norton and ignored the criticism. Only as he jogged back upfield did he glance warily towards the spectator as the heckling continued.

'Want to borrow some specs, ref?'

There were a few giggles from children nearby, but not many other people in the crowd found the remark very funny. They agreed with the referee that the girl's shot had slithered wide without anyone touching it.

Mr Jones, on the opposite touchline, was far from amused. He knew he might have to take some action soon and put a stop to such nonsense before it affected the players.

Danebridge had made a bright start to the cup-tie. Rakesh had already forced the goalkeeper to make a save and fired another effort just over the crossbar. And now Kerry had gone close too. She was desperate for the team to win today so that she could play in the Final.

'Good try, Kerry!' came Chris's cry of encouragement from the edge of his penalty area. 'We're getting warmer.'

The goal-kick was sliced and Kerry pounced on the loose ball, lofting it back towards goal while the keeper was still out of position. He stumbled and could only watch its flight helplessly, but the ball sailed just a little too high. It thudded against the bar and rebounded down into the boy's arms as he knelt on the ground, as if in prayer.

Gasps of dismay and relief rippled around the touchline from the two sets of supporters before a single voice stood out.

'That's two you've missed inside thirty seconds, girl. You're useless! You shouldn't be on the pitch.'

'You've no right to say something like that,' Mum objected. 'She didn't do it on purpose.'

'Keep your thoughts to yourself, Tony,' Grandad told him sternly. 'That young lass is a fine player.'

He only laughed. 'I don't agree with girls playing football, Pop. Shouldn't be allowed.'

'Shut up, Dad,' Andrew hissed. 'You're not helping. Grandad's right, Kerry's good. She's well worth her place in the team.'

Kerry would have been flabbergasted to hear Andrew sticking up for her. As it was, she glared at the man next to him, wishing that looks could kill. It took all her self control not to shout something rude back.

'Who does that clown in the black jacket think he is?' she stormed at Rakesh. 'Is he one of their lot?'

Rakesh shook his head. 'One of ours, I'm afraid. Hard to believe, but I gather he's Chris's dad.'

'Right!' she answered as realization dawned. 'The guy who went and put Chris off in the league match.'

'That's the one. Nice bloke, eh, by the sound of it!'

It was Danebridge's turn now to do some defending as Great Norton mounted their first raid on Chris's goal. Philip's challenge for the ball was powerful enough to make an attacker lose control before he could shoot – and also lose his balance. The collision of bodies was just outside the penalty area and the referee blew for a direct free-kick.

'That was never a foul!' Dad

screamed. 'The kid fell over his own clumsy feet. You're blind, referee!'

The official shot him a dirty look. 'I'm reffing this game, not you.'

'Yes, and a right mess you're making of it too,' he retorted.

The free-kick was a beauty. The ball was hooked over the defensive wall and slapped into the net well beyond Chris's dive. He had no hope of reaching it in the large recky goals.

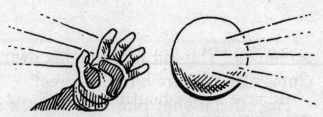

His dad was enraged. 'Rubbish, Danebridge! So sloppy. C'mon, Chris, sort your players out. Show 'em who's boss!'

'Don't start on at Chris, Dad,' pleaded Andrew. 'That's not fair.'

Andrew spotted Mr Jones striding round the pitch in their direction. 'Oh, oh!' he muttered under his breath. 'Here comes trouble...'

The headmaster didn't even see Ryan's flying header. Danebridge had almost equalized instantly as Rakesh sped down the wing and curled over a low centre into the goalmouth. It was a wonderful effort from Ryan, the ball flashing only a fraction wide of the far post, but Dad was still cursing another missed chance when he found he had company.

'Please stop shouting things out, Mr Weston,' the headmaster demanded. 'You're embarrassing everybody and making a fool of yourself too.'

'Oh really. It's a free country, isn't it?' he snapped. 'Or at least it was when I left.'

Mum cut in. 'Yes, and I think it's about time you took off again. You're showing us all up.'

His wife's response had the desired effect. It silenced him at last – if only for a while...

Great Norton dominated the rest of the first half, eagerly seeking to increase their 1-0 lead. They were now playing with much more confidence than Danebridge, who seemed to have gone into their shell like a nervous tortoise.

Chris was especially jittery, afraid that any mistake would be picked up by Dad and broadcast to the world. He fumbled a couple of shots he would normally have held comfortably and then dropped a cross at the feet of an attacker. The ball was poked goalwards but Philip scrambled to his captain's rescue by kicking it off the line.

Chris waited for the expected blast and was amazed when it failed to come. He knew Dad was still there. He could see him alongside Mr Jones.

His luck didn't last. Goalkeeping errors are usually costly and so it proved just before the interval. Chris dashed out from his goal to try and catch a corner and mistimed his jump for the ball. It swirled over his

flailing hands and an attacker lurking behind him steered it into the net.

Dad could no longer restrain himself. 'Rubbish, Chris! Get a grip, lad!' he yelled. 'You're letting people down.'

Mr Jones was furious. 'You're the one letting people down, Mr Weston. I must ask you to leave immediately.'

For an awful moment Andrew thought his dad was going to lash out at the headmaster. Dad was clearly having a struggle to control his temper.

'This is a public recreation ground, not your school,' he snarled, refusing to budge. 'I'll stay here as long as I want.'

Shoot sensed the angry mood of the people around him and began barking as Grandad stepped in and put a hand on his son-in-law's arm.

'Time to go,' he said simply, but in a manner that made it plain he meant business. 'Let's have a cup of tea and a chat in my cottage.'

Dad reacted strongly. He snatched his arm away and caught Grandad accidentally across the chest, making him stagger backwards. His cap fell to the ground and only Mum's firm grip on the lead prevented Shoot from launching at her husband.

Andrew did so instead. 'Cool it, Dad!' he cried, yanking him away by his other arm. 'That's enough. You've gone too far.'

His dad suddenly deflated like a burst balloon, shocked that even Andrew had turned against him. He

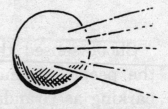

tried to recover some of his lost dignity, pulling his jacket back into shape and straightening his tie.

'Wasting my time here anyway, watching this shower,' he snorted as a parting shot to Mr Jones. 'They've thrown it away. Danebridge have got no chance now.'

'We might have without you here, Dad,' said Andrew. 'C'mon, let's go.'

6 No Hard Feelings

The half-time whistle blew as Grandad ushered Andrew and his dad into the kitchen. 'Sit down at the table, both of you, while I put the kettle on,' he said. 'We need to have a good talk together.'

So did the Danebridge team. They were losing 2-0, just as against Shenby, and the players rallied round their unhappy captain.

'Nobody's blaming you, Chris,' Philip reassured him. 'You can't help what your dad's like.'

'He's gone now, anyway,' Kerry said. 'Good riddance too!'

'Yeah, just forget about him,' said Rakesh.

Chris wished it was that easy, but at least he tried to shut Dad out of his mind for the moment. 'C'mon, let's put things right where it matters – on the pitch,' he urged his teammates. 'We can still win this game.'

Danebridge staged a spirited comeback at the start of the second half and found the net themselves at last. Kerry set the goal up by dribbling past two defenders and Ryan scored it. As she lost possession of the ball in another challenge, it ran free to Ryan, who squeezed his shot beneath the keeper's dive.

For a while it looked as though an

equalizer was on the cards. Rakesh struck a post and Great Norton were fortunate to withstand several minutes of heavy pressure. Then they caught Danebridge on the break.

The visitors' third goal was almost an exact copy of Danebridge's winner against Hanfield in the previous round. A swift raid up the right wing left Philip having to deal with two pacy opponents at the same time. He couldn't cope and Chris soon had the equally thankless task of picking the ball out of the net.

The semi-final appeared to be all over. And it would have been, too, if Chris hadn't remained alert. Despite the 3-1 scoreline, he felt more relaxed and positive than at any stage in the game, free of further off-field distractions. In a strange sense, Danebridge now had nothing to lose.

'Push forward,' the captain called from the edge of his penalty area. 'All-out attack. We're not gonna be knocked out without a fight.'

The brave tactics nearly backfired immediately. A move broke down after a weak pass and the ball was

punted deep into unguarded Danebridge territory. It even went over the head of Philip, the tallest player on the pitch. As Great Norton's two fastest strikers held a sprint race to see who could reach the ball first, neither of them won. They were beaten to it by Chris, acting as sweeper, who had zoomed out of his area to hack the ball into touch.

'Didn't know you were so quick,' laughed Rakesh.

Chris grinned. 'You'll have to watch out on Sports Day this year!'

The goalkeeper had to repeat his frantic charge out of goal a little later, but this time he miskicked and the winger kept the ball in play. Although Philip delayed the boy's shot long enough for Chris to hare back, the high lob seemed certain to clinch Great Norton's victory.

No-one was quite sure how Chris managed to recover his position in time to fingertip the ball over the bar, but his acrobatics had the crowd gasping. Chris finished up entangled in the netting, too dazed and winded to appreciate the generous applause that rang around the recreation ground.

Danebridge took inspiration from their captain's heroics. They bombarded Great Norton with attack after attack and their opponents eventually cracked in the blitz of raids. Two goals came in three minutes.

Ryan made both of them, slipping accurate passes through the gaps in their defence to allow Rakesh and then Kerry to fire home and bring the scores level at 3-3. The cup-tie had a thrilling climax as Great Norton hung

on for dear life, grateful to survive until the final whistle

'There goes my chance to play in the Final,' sighed Kerry, sitting exhausted on the penalty spot afterwards. 'I bet we won't be able to fit it in now before Easter.'

'We've got to win the replay first,' Rakesh reminded her.

'Oh, we will,' she said confidently. 'I'm sure we'd have won today but for you-know-who. That stupid bloke's gone and cost me my medal!'

Chris was willing to be more forgiving, if only because he realized that Dad's behaviour had helped to bring the best out of his team in the end. Some of the things they'd heard Dad saying had spurred them on even more, determined to prove him wrong.

He collected his clothes from the

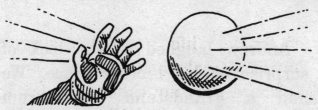

hut without bothering to change and followed Mum and Shoot to Grandad's cottage.

'I'm really proud of you,' Mum said. 'It was lovely when everybody was clapping and cheering after that save of yours.'

Chris smiled. 'I'm glad you didn't see us lose, Mum, but it's a shame Dad wasn't there as well. He won't believe how we fought back like that.'

Dad already knew. He'd watched the last part of the game with Andrew and Grandad from a bedroom window and they were all in the kitchen again when Chris opened the door.

'Well played, son,' Dad greeted him. 'Terrific save!'

Andrew laughed at the look of surprise on his brother's face. 'We had a grandstand view from upstairs,' he explained. 'Like being in one of those executive boxes at a soccer stadium.'

'The only problem is, we don't know the final score,' said Grandad. 'You can't have lost, surely, the way people were jumping about.'

Chris shook his head. 'Draw, three each. Replay in a fortnight.'

Dad cleared his throat. 'Er, you'll be pleased to know that I won't be able to spoil things for you then,' he said with a lopsided grin. 'I'm returning to Spain next week.'

'On his own,' Grandad added quickly, as Chris glanced at Andrew.

'I wasn't really planning on going, anyway,' he said, trying to sound casual. 'I'd miss everybody here too

much – even you, our kid!'

Shoot wandered over to sit at Dad's side, yawned and waited to be stroked. 'Typical!' grunted Dad, tickling the dog's ears. 'Shoot's decided we can be friends now that I'm leaving.'

'Perhaps he doesn't see you as a threat any more,' said Mum. 'It'd be nice if we could all try and be friends again.'

'Even join you in Spain for a holiday?' suggested Andrew hopefully.

'You'd be very welcome to,' Dad said. 'No hard feelings, eh, Chris? Sorry about my big mouth.'

'No hard feelings, Dad,' Chris replied, smiling. 'At least my team know it's big enough for them to make you eat all your words!'

Dad laughed loudly. 'And I know that Danebridge have got a top class keeper. Their future's in safe hands – so long as I'm not around!'

Shoot slumped down at their feet, curled up and dozed off. Some things in life, seemed to be his message, were far more important than what happened on a football field – even during a cup semi-final!

THE END

ROB CHILDS
THE BIG DROP

Illustrated by Jon Riley

For all young Asian footballers

1 Relegation Battle

'No sweat!' exclaimed Rakesh. 'All we have to do is beat Ashford and we'll be OK, look!'

'I'm trying to, if you'd shift out the way a bit so the rest of us can see,' said Chris, shuffling for position among the footballers clustered around the sports noticeboard.

The latest league table did not make happy viewing for Chris Weston, neither as goalkeeper nor team captain of Danebridge Primary School.

It gave him a painful reminder that he had already let in 28 goals this season. And it also showed Danebridge in the wrong half – third from bottom out of nine schools.

	P	W	D	L	Goals F	A	Pts
League table –bottom three . . .							
Danebridge	13	3	3	7	19	28	12
Brentway	14	2	4	8	16	35	10
Ashford	14	2	3	9	20	37	9

'At least we still have three matches left to play,' put in Philip, who was tall enough to study the table from the back of the group. 'The others have only got two.'

'Just as well,' Chris muttered. 'We might need that game in hand, if we go

and mess things up against Ashford
tomorrow.'

'We won't do that,' Rakesh assured
him. 'Anyway, even getting one more
point from a draw would be good
enough to make us safe – right?'

'Well, just about, but not mathematically.'

'You sound like the Professor,'
chuckled the striker, referring to a
teammate who was also a genius with

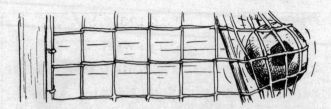

numbers – something Rakesh would never pretend to be. 'I thought we had a better goal difference than Ashford.'

'We do – but if they had a big win, everything could change.'

'Good job only one team goes down, then, I reckon,' said Philip.

'Yeah, so long as it's not us who end up getting the chop.'

Danebridge's headmaster gathered the players together before the kick-off at Ashford next day.

'It's up to you,' he stressed. 'Your fate's in your own hands – and feet.'

Mr Jones didn't bother to mention their heads. He could barely recall anyone scoring a headed goal apart from Philip, in a cup match.

'You've done very well to recover after losing the first four games of the season,' he praised them. 'Another three points for a victory today and you can forget any relegation fears.'

Rakesh started the match as if he intended to win it all by himself. For a time, it was almost a one-man show.

Danebridge's leading scorer fired in four shots on target in quick succession. He hit the goalkeeper once, the woodwork twice and finally found the net with a crisp half-volley from the edge of the penalty area.

Only then did he allow somebody else in on the act – a girl. Rakesh swept across a perfect centre for his strike

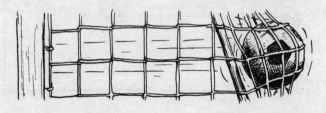

partner to slide home the second goal at the far post. All Kerry had to do was tap the ball over the line.

'Thanks, Rakky,' she smiled, jumping up to slap his raised hand in celebration. 'You put it on a plate for me. I couldn't miss.'

'Plenty more where that came from,' he grinned. 'This lot are useless. No wonder they're bottom of the league.'

The shock of going 2–0 down in this vital relegation battle seemed to wake Ashford up. Either that or the Danebridge players dozed off in the spring sunshine, dreaming of helping themselves to a feast of goals whenever they felt hungry.

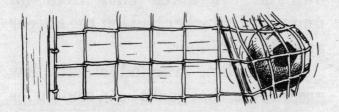

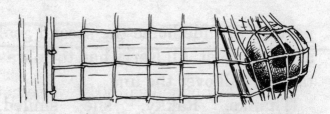

As Danebridge eased up, they failed to heed the danger signs that the home side were beginning to find their form and putting together some promising moves. Even after Chris had been forced to make an acrobatic save, the captain's anxious warnings fell upon deaf ears.

'C'mon, team, get a grip!' he urged. 'We're giving them too much space.'

It came as no surprise to the spectators when a grumbling Chris soon had to fish the ball out of the back of his own net. A fierce shot from an unmarked attacker had left the keeper groping at thin air.

His watching grandad let out a low groan. 'Aye, that goal's been coming for a while. I could feel it in my aching bones.'

Mr Jones nodded sadly. 'If we're not careful, we're going to throw this match away.'

The headmaster changed the team formation during the interval, using two substitutes, but it was to no avail. The second half was a total disaster.

It began in dramatic fashion with penalties at both ends.

Tripped as he was about to shoot, Rakesh insisted on taking the penalty himself and blazed the kick wildly over the crossbar. Two minutes later, the Professor handled the ball in attempting to clear a corner and the referee pointed to the spot again.

Unfortunately, Chris didn't have the luxury of seeing the ball sail over the bar. Ashford's penalty was aimed low for the bottom left-hand corner of his goal. He guessed correctly and dived full-length, but the kick had too much power. It brushed past his outstretched arm to level the scores at 2–2.

After that, things went from bad to worse. Danebridge wasted several chances to regain the lead before conceding a soft third goal against the run of play.

Ashford's number nine bustled through Philip's clumsy challenge and shot from a narrow angle, off balance. The ball took a slight deflection off another defender's boot and somehow squeezed over the line between Chris and his near post. It proved a costly error.

At the final whistle, the dejected captain made a brave effort to call out 'Three Cheers' for their opponents, but the response from his teammates was half-hearted. They knew they had blown it – and also that they had only themselves to blame for the disastrous 3–2 defeat.

As the Danebridge players trudged

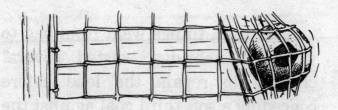

off the pitch, they tried to avoid looking one another in the eye. They were too busy staring relegation full in the face.

2 Ups and Downs

'Knew you lot would go down this season without me in the team.'

Rakesh ignored the voice behind him in the lunch queue and carried on discussing the match. 'If only I'd scored that penalty, the result might have been different.'

'Not your fault we lost. I'd have been too nervous even to take it,' admitted Philip.

'Guess that's why I missed it. I knew how much was at stake . . .'

He was interrupted again. 'The reason you missed it, Patel, was 'cos you're rubbish!'

Rakesh turned round to confront Luke Bradshaw. 'What's it got to do with you? Nothing!'

Luke smirked at them. 'Got some news you might like to hear.'

'Doubt it.'

'Do you want the good news or the bad?'

'Is the good news that you're leaving?' asked Philip cheekily. Although he was a year younger than Luke, he was already taller, and felt safe that the bully would think twice about taking him on.

'No such luck,' Luke sneered. 'Wish I could get out of this dump and go somewhere that recognized my talents.'

Luke had never forgiven the headmaster for banning him from playing football for the school after causing trouble earlier in the season.

'Didn't know you had any talents,' said Rakesh, deliberately goading him. The two of them barely spoke to one another usually, apart from trading insults.

'Don't push yer luck, Patel,' snarled Luke, his fists clenching. 'Bet you didn't know either that Brentway won yesterday as well.'

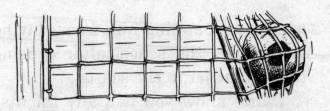

'I don't believe you. You're just making it up.'

Luke shrugged. 'Suit yourself. I know a kid who goes there. Perhaps you'll believe dear old Jonesy when he gets round to tellin' you.'

'So what's the good news, then?' asked Philip as Luke moved off to push in the queue nearer the front.

'That *is* the good news, stupid,' he called back over his shoulder. 'At least to me it is. It means you're now level bottom with Ashford.'

He began to taunt them with a tuneless chant, annoying everyone else around him too. *'Goin' down . . . goin' down . . . goin' down . . .'*

*

After school, Chris kept a weekly date with Kerry – on horseback!

At the start of term, the captain had found a way to persuade sharpshooter Kerry to play for the school team. He bet her that she couldn't score goals in a proper football match like she did every Monday afternoon in Games. She took up the challenge and he lost the bet – both as expected.

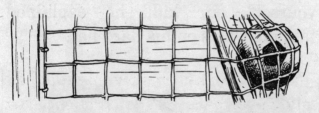

Today was the day for Chris to fulfil his side of the bargain – that he would learn to ride well enough to attempt a jump. Time was running out for him to do so. The team was still recovering from the shock of hearing that Kerry would be leaving soon. Her parents were going to open a new riding school in another county.

The event was drawing a crowd. Several of the players turned up to watch, and so had Grandad and Chris's older brother.

Andrew had come straight from school, still in the uniform of Selworth Comprehensive. 'Couldn't miss the chance of seeing you make a fool of yourself, our kid,' he explained, tapping Chris on his hard hat.

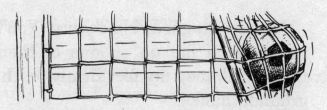

Chris pulled a face. 'Should've known. You have a habit of popping up at just the wrong time.'

'Charming! And here's me ready to run to your rescue,' he sniggered. 'I've brought a load of safety pins and Sellotape to stick you back together again after you fall off!'

'Don't hold your breath. Kerry says there's nothing to it. The pony does most of the work.'

Andrew gazed towards the stables. 'Which one's yours? That great big black brute?'

'No, the little chestnut.'

'Ah! How sweet!' Andrew cooed sarcastically. 'My little pony.'

'I'd like to see you ride it.'

Andrew laughed. 'No chance! You'll never catch me up on one of them things. I'll keep my feet firmly on the ground, thanks.'

'Well, then, you shouldn't mock,' said Grandad. 'Chris has done very well in just a few lessons.'

'I was dead nervous when I first got on,' Chris admitted, 'but riding's great fun. Might decide to keep it up, even after Kerry's gone.'

He discovered that Kerry's mother, the instructor, was taking his group of beginners on a short hack around a couple of fields before returning to the school paddock to practise jumping. Kerry went with them to help, riding her favourite palomino pony.

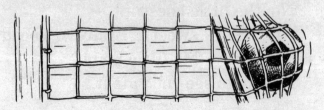

As they changed from a walk to a trot, Kerry moved up alongside Chris. 'Relax, keep well balanced,' she advised. 'Feel the rhythm, sit and rise, sit and rise – that's it, good.'

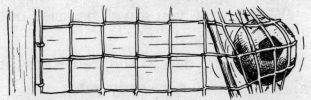

Chris grinned. 'Think I might be catching this riding bug, just like you've done with soccer.'

'At least it takes your mind off relegation for a while.'

'Right – the only big drop I'm worried about at the moment is falling off when we start jumping.'

'Falling doesn't bother me,' Kerry said with a laugh. 'It's hitting the ground that hurts!'

As the ponies completed a circuit of the first field, they broke into a canter.

Seeing Andrew and the others leaning against the fence, Chris felt a sudden surge of bravado. He noticed an old rotten log lying in the grass not far away and turned towards it.

'Watch this, you guys!' he cried out. 'This is how to do it.'

'No, Chris, don't!' shouted Kerry in alarm. 'You're not ready yet.'

It was too late. Chris could not have stopped the pony now even if he'd wanted to – which he did. His confidence of a few moments ago had totally deserted him.

He did the right thing by instinct, leaning forward as the pony jumped the log, but failed to straighten up again on landing. The jolt threw him further forward, his feet came out of the stirrups and he lost hold of the reins too. Chris grabbed the pony's mane to try and save himself, then

wrapped his arms around its neck and clung on for all he was worth. Within a few strides, however, he slid down one side and was bumped off into the long grass.

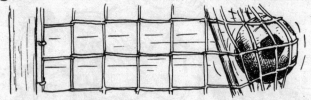

Kerry was the first to reach him, dismounting quickly to check that he was all right. Chris was too winded to speak and had no defence against her scolding tongue once she was sure there was no damage done.

'Idiot! What did you go and do a crazy thing like that for?' she complained. 'Showing off in front of your mates. Typical!'

Andrew only just beat Grandad over the fence and they arrived on the scene as Chris was getting shakily to his feet. 'Didn't know that was how it was supposed to be done, little brother,' he teased.

'It's not,' Kerry snapped. 'He's just taking after his big brother for a change – acting stupid!'

'Oh dear! She's cross. You won't get a gold star now, our kid,' he grinned as Kerry sprang up into her saddle.

'Well, c'mon, then,' she ordered. 'No good feeling sorry for yourself. Mum's got your pony so go and get back on. The lesson's not over yet.'

Grandad was rather more sympathetic and helped Chris to brush himself down. 'Looks like you've learnt one thing already, m'boy,' he said with a chuckle.

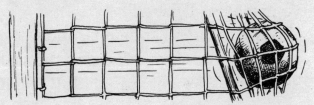

'What's that, Grandad?' he said sheepishly.

'The truth of the old saying: *Pride comes before a fall*!'

Chris nodded. 'I think we all found that out for ourselves in the Ashford match,' he said, sighing. 'And now I'll be making doubly sure we won't make that kind of mistake again.'

3 Seeing Red

'Good save, Rakky!' cried Kerry. 'We'll have to play you in goal next game.'

Rakesh grinned. He was well pleased with the stop he'd just made to prevent her scoring. 'Nah , think I'll let Chris keep his job. He's a better goalie than he is a show-jumper!'

Making jokes at the captain's expense had given them all plenty of laughs over the past few days, but Chris took the ribbing in good heart. In a funny sort of way, it seemed to have

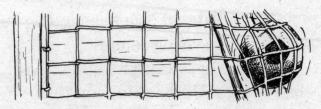

helped lift everyone's spirits again after the Ashford defeat.

Kerry didn't normally join in the lunchtime kickabout with the other footballers. She preferred to play with her own friends. But she found herself increasingly caught up with the team's efforts to do the double – to escape relegation and win the Cup. Danebridge still had a semi-final game to look forward to and Kerry was keen to reach the Final, even if she would not be around after Easter to take part in it.

As the action switched to the other end of their short pitch where Chris was in goal, Rakesh didn't see Luke sidle up behind him.

'Fancy yourself as a keeper, do you?' came the sneering remark.

'Not really,' Rakesh replied with a heavy sigh. 'Just taking my turn.'

Luke kicked out in spite at the cast-off clothes that made up one of the posts, scattering them about.

'Clear off, will you,' Rakesh snapped, rebuilding the pile. 'You know we don't want you here.'

'Huh! Put you off, do I? Just 'cos you all know I'm the best player in the school.'

'There's only you who thinks that. We lost every game you played in.'

'That was stupid old Jonesy's fault, not mine. He should never have picked Weston as captain.'

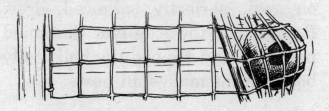

'Good decision, if you ask me.'

'I'm not askin' you,' Luke scoffed. 'Look what's happened without me. Things are so bad, Jonesy's even had to start pickin' girls!'

'Belt up, Bradshaw,' Rakesh said wearily, tired of such a pointless argument. 'Kerry's a great goal-scorer. If you can't see that, you must be blind.'

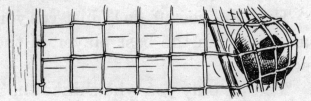

Just at that moment, as if intent on proving his point, Kerry broke away with the ball. She kept it under full control as she advanced rapidly on goal, perfectly balanced, drew Rakesh out towards her, dummied past him and slipped the ball coolly between the makeshift posts.

'Anybody else want to go in goal?' Rakesh shouted out. 'There's a bad smell hanging round there.'

Something flew past his head. He didn't know whether it was a stone or a piece of dirt. He whirled round to confront his tormentor.

'Watch it! You do that again and I'll . . .'

'You'll do what?' Luke cackled. 'Accuse me of racism?'

'The colour of my skin's got nothing to do with it,' Rakesh fumed.

'Oh, yeah? Well, this is what I think of you people then . . .'

Luke began to spout a torrent of racial abuse aimed at Rakesh and his family. The next thing the players knew, Rakesh had launched himself at Luke and the two boys were wrestling on the ground.

'Fight! Fight!' went up the shout.

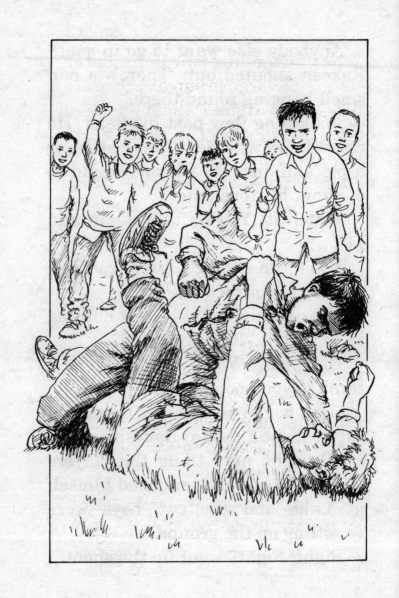

The pummelling pair immediately attracted a large group of onlookers, all circling around them to get a better view. By the time Chris arrived, there was already blood splattered about, but it wasn't clear whose nose or mouth it was coming from.

'C'mon, help me,' Chris cried out. 'We've got to break it up.'

Philip waded in with the captain to try and pull the fighters apart and a wayward fist thumped Chris on the shoulder. Two lunchtime supervisors dashed up to put a stop to the free-for-all and sent six children, including Kerry, into school to see the headmaster.

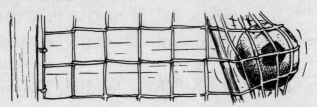

'Going at it like a bunch of wild hooligans, they were,' one of the women reported to Mr Jones.

'And such terrible language too,' added the other.

'Right, thank you, ladies,' he said grimly. 'This is a very serious matter. Just leave it to me now. I'll deal with it.'

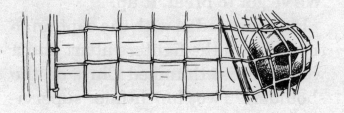

Luke Bradshaw was sent home in disgrace and also suspended from school for the rest of term.

'Good riddance!' was the general reaction to his punishment, but the footballers were more concerned about Rakesh. Their leading scorer had been dropped from the next league fixture, Danebridge's crucial last home match of the season.

'I don't think it's fair,' said Chris that evening in Grandad's cottage, telling him about what had happened. 'I mean, Jonesy knows why the fight started. Kerry spoke up for Rakesh. She heard what Bradshaw said to him.'

'Nasty piece of work, that Luke Bradshaw, by all accounts,' replied Grandad. 'The boy may well find himself in more hot water yet over this business, but your headmaster was in an awkward position today. He could hardly have let Rakesh off scot-free, however bad the provocation.'

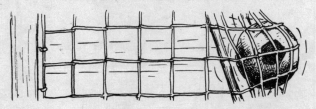

Chris pulled a face. 'Well, Jonesy won't be able to complain if we go and lose now after banning his main striker.'

'Football's a team game,' said Grandad. 'Rakesh isn't the only one who can put the ball in the back of the net, you know. It gives other people a chance now to show what they can do.'

Chris didn't seem convinced. 'I just can't stand the thought of Luke going around bragging that he helped to get us relegated.'

'You'll be OK, m'boy,' Grandad assured him. 'Sounds to me like that's all the motivation the team will need to do well against Highgate.'

'Hope you're right. We've already won 2–0 away at their place so they'll be out for revenge.'

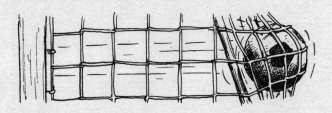

'I remember that game. It was your first win this season.'

'Yes, but do you also remember who scored both our goals? Rakesh!'

4 Three's a Crowd

'C'mon, the Reds!' cried Rakesh as the striped shirts of Danebridge kicked off against the all-white strip of Highgate Juniors.

Rakesh was among the spectators, eager to play a part by cheering the team to a victory that would put them three points clear of Ashford again. His one consolation in missing this game – apart from giving Luke Bradshaw a black eye – was that at least he'd be able to play on Saturday at Selworth, his previous school. He was desperate to do well against his old mates.

Grandad did not have far to travel to see his favourite team in action – just a short walk down his garden path on to the village recreation ground. He soon sensed how nervous the players must be feeling. They could barely string two passes together.

'Good job we're not up against a better team than Highgate, by the look of things,' Grandad grunted to himself. 'They're just as bad as we are.'

It was certainly not the best game that he had ever watched on the recky. If it had been on television, he would have either switched over, turned off or gone to sleep. The dismal first half proved goal-less, but that situation changed immediately after the restart.

A miskick in midfield and poor marking in defence allowed a Highgate attacker a clear run at goal. Chris came out to narrow the shooting angle, but the ball was lobbed over his head and just underneath the crossbar.

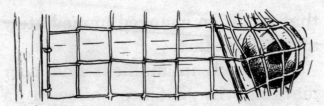

As Chris trailed back to scoop the ball out of the netting, he noticed a figure saunter over the footbridge across the River Dane. 'Oh, great, that's all we need,' he groaned. 'Bradshaw's come to gloat.'

Luke checked the score with a spectator before stopping behind the goal. 'Losin', are we?' he smirked. 'What a shame!'

'Didn't think you'd dare show your ugly face here,' Chris replied.

'Huh! Jonesy can't stop me comin' on the recky. Nobody can.'

'You want a bet on that?' said Chris, nodding at another newcomer who suddenly appeared at Luke's side.

'Time to go home, I reckon, Bradshaw.'

The harsh voice made him jump.

'I only just got here,' he protested.

'So have I. And you know what they say – three's a crowd . . .'

Luke took the hint. He slouched away back to the bridge without even making any other snide comments to annoy Chris. He could tell the older boy meant business.

'. . . and two's company, eh? Just you and me now, our kid.'

'Thanks, Andrew,' Chris smiled. 'I take back what I said last week. You timed your arrival just right for once.'

Andrew smirked. 'Anything else I

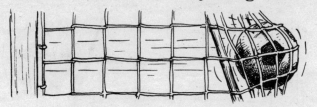

can do for my little brother? I've got my boots with me if you need a supersub.'

'Sorry, we'll have to manage without you somehow. You're too old!'

'Yeah, guess their teacher might object,' Andrew laughed. 'But Jonesy must be wishing he could bring Rakky on now, eh?'

Rakesh was doing his best to help. He'd spent the whole match shouting advice and encouragement.

'Play it wide, Professor,' he screamed as Danebridge launched an attack in search of the equalizer. 'Give it to Ryan. He's got loads of space.'

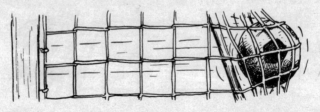

Mark Towers, alias the Professor, must have heard him. Or perhaps it was simply his boots obeying their master. The absent-minded Professor had left his own at home – not for the first time – and had borrowed Rakesh's pair.

Ryan was running free along the right touchline and took Mark's pass in his stride. The young winger had time to look up and pick out a target for his cross, spotting just the one he wanted – Kerry.

His centre wasn't as accurate as he might have liked, though, and Kerry had to check back to gain possession. It allowed a defender to charge down her delayed shot and the ball rebounded out of the danger area. Or at least that's what the Highgate goalkeeper thought.

Mark had wandered forward in

support of the attack and the ball sat up perfectly for him, almost begging to be hit. So he granted its wish and walloped the ball as hard as he could. It flew out of the keeper's reach and snicked the inside of the post on its way into the net.

'Magic boots, Rakky!' he cried, waving across to him.

Rakesh grinned. 'Bradshaw might have got me banned, but he couldn't stop my boots from scoring!'

The last ten exciting minutes made up for the rest of the drab match as Danebridge pressed hard for the winning goal. Kerry went closest with a volley that skimmed over the bar, although Ryan might have grabbed the glory for himself if he'd kept a cooler head. His hurried shot was poked tamely straight at the goalkeeper.

In the end, Danebridge had to be grateful that their captain stayed alert and on his toes. Chris had to sprint from his area to snuff out the threat of a late Highgate raid by kicking the ball away almost into the river.

The 1–1 draw gave the Reds a precious point, but their relief was only temporary. The next day, they were dismayed to see on the notice-board that Brentway remained above them in the league table. It was clear that any of the bottom three schools could still be relegated.

	P	W	D	L	Goals F	A	Pts
Brentway	16	3	5	8	20	38	14
Danebridge	15	3	4	8	22	32	13
Ashford	15	3	3	9	23	39	12

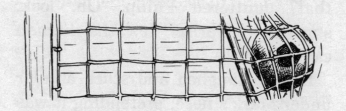

'Brentway must have got a draw too,' Philip groaned.

'Yeah, but they've run out of games,' said Rakesh. 'They can only sweat it out now, hoping that either us or Ashford slip up.'

'Who are Ashford playing?'

It was Chris that answered. 'Highgate at home, so we can't rely on that lot doing us any favours. I bet Ashford will beat them, just like we should have done.'

'It all comes down to mathematics,' piped up a voice behind them. 'Most things do in the end.'

'Now I wonder who could have said

that?' muttered Philip. 'Oh, look, surprise, surprise! It's the human calculator!'

Rakesh laughed and stuck a ruler under Mark's nose, pretending it was a microphone. 'We're lucky to have the Professor here in the studio, listeners. Perhaps he can explain the situation to us. Professor, what exactly do Danebridge have to do to stay up?'

Mark pulled a face, but went along with the game. He could never resist having an audience.

'Well, listeners, it's basically quite simple,' he began. 'Danebridge have a superior goal difference to both their rivals, so only need another point to make certain of survival. And they could even afford to lose against Selworth so long as Ashford didn't win their game. Now this is where it starts to get really interesting mathematically – because if Ashford . . .'

Rakesh snatched the microphone away quickly. 'Yes, thank you, Professor. Very interesting, I'm sure, but that's all we have time for at the moment. Now over to the weather forecast . . .'

'Anyway, it's no use thinking about what Ashford might do,' said Chris. 'They're playing on Saturday as well so we won't even know their result.'

'Yes, we will,' Mark grinned. 'My dad will be there. He's going to keep ringing Mum on the mobile to relay the score.'

'Tell him he needn't bother, 'cos we're gonna thrash Selworth,' Rakesh boasted. 'I've promised them a hat-trick!'

The captain wished he could be so optimistic. Selworth had already beaten Danebridge 5–1, their heaviest defeat of the season.

5 On the Attack

'I've been thinking,' said Chris as the players went over the footbridge onto the recky for their regular Thursday practice session. 'It's a bit like when I fell off that pony.'

Philip paused to gaze down into the rippling water of the river below to see if he could spot any fish. He couldn't. He never did, but he always stopped to look. 'What – still sore, you mean?'

'No! Are you listening? I'm talking about our poor form in the league.'

'Yeah, right . . . er . . . why is that like falling off a pony?'

'Well, we've got to pick ourselves up and try to do better, just like I had to last week,' Chris explained.

'We sure need to play a lot better this time against Selworth. A draw's about the best we can hope for, I reckon.'

'Maybe, but it's too risky just playing for a draw. It could be curtains if they went and scored a late goal to beat us,' Chris said. 'We've got to be positive and go there looking for a win.'

Mr Jones must have agreed. He set up one of their favourite practice games – attack versus defence. The attackers earned points for every effort at goal, plus a bonus if they scored, while the defenders gained points for clearing the ball over the halfway line.

The defence was soon on top. They built up a useful early lead and made the attacking players work hard to create any decent chances. Rakesh had the first shot on target, but saw it deflected away by Philip for a corner. Ryan took it, swinging the ball into the goalmouth where Chris leapt high to snatch it clean off Rakesh's head.

Heading was not their strong point. The strikers were all small, nippy players who preferred having the ball at their feet rather than up in the air. They had little hope of outjumping tall defenders and goalkeepers. The next swift attack, however, provided a perfect example of their strengths.

Ryan and Rakesh exchanged neat passes to carve open the defence before Rakesh slipped the ball through to Kerry. It was a killer pass. Left with just Philip to beat, Kerry almost tied his long legs in knots as she dummied one way and then the other. He had no idea what she was going to do next.

Neither did Chris. When the shot was finally unleashed, it caught him

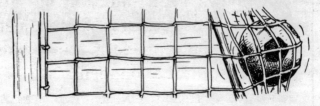

wrong-footed and the keeper could only watch the ball whizz past into the goal. In a sense, he was pleased. It was good to see Kerry so sharp again – and it was great to have Rakesh back too. They were going to need them both on top form on Saturday.

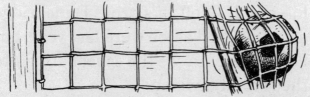

'Good luck, our kid,' said Andrew as he and Chris clambered out of Grandad's car outside Selworth School. 'Hope Danebridge stay up.'

'Do you really mean that?'

'Course I do.'

'But you've been taunting me all season about us getting relegated, just like Luke. You've made it sound like you really want it to happen.'

Andrew grinned. 'Nah, you know

me. Only pulling your leg.'

'C'mon, be honest. I bet you'll be secretly pleased if we go down, just so you can say the team's rubbish since you left.'

Andrew's grin turned somewhat sheepish, knowing that Chris had read his mind. 'Well, it's true, Danebridge aren't as good as we were last year, but I'd still hate to see the school drop into the second division.'

Grandad interrupted. 'Anyway, whatever happens today, it's not the end of the world.'

'It's not even the end of the season,' Chris added. 'We've still got a big cup match to play next week, remember.'

'Just make sure your team concentrate on this one first,' Grandad chuckled. 'You know what they say in football – take each game as it comes.'

Danebridge started this game in great style. After mounting a series of dangerous attacks, the Reds put the ball in the Selworth net.

'What a goal!' cried Rakesh. 'Keeper never moved!'

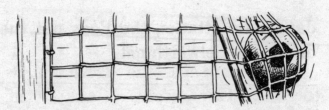

His delight was short-lived. He'd just leapt onto the scorer's back, toppling Ryan to the ground, when the referee's repeated blasts on the whistle made him realize that something was wrong.

'No goal,' announced Selworth's teacher. 'Free-kick to the Blues.'

Rakesh scrambled to his feet first and stared at the referee in disbelief. He hadn't seen any foul before Ryan crashed the ball home, and nobody could have been offside. A defender had been standing on the goal line.

'Sorry, Rakesh,' said the referee. 'It was handball.'

If it had been anyone else, Rakesh might have made a protest, but he knew the referee well. Mr Carter had once been his class teacher.

Ryan confirmed the decision was correct. 'He's right, Rakky,' he admitted. 'The ball bounced up and hit my hand before I shot.'

Five minutes later, the visitors suffered a further setback. There was a goal at the other end, and this one counted. Danebridge failed to clear a corner properly and the ball was stabbed past Chris from close range.

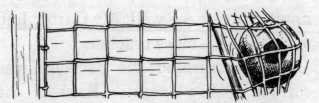

What made it worse for Rakesh was that the scorer was his best mate at Selworth, a lad that he still played with for a Sunday League side. After his noisy celebrations, Dinesh made sure that he caught his friend's eye.

'Wicked goal, eh, Rakky?' he cackled.

'Huh! Goalhanging, as usual,' Rakesh retorted, unimpressed. 'We'll see who has the last laugh.'

There wasn't much for Danebridge to laugh about in the first half.

Ryan and Kerry hit good chances over the bar, Rakesh hooked another into the side netting and Mark had to limp off with a leg injury. The mood in the camp at half-time would have been even more grim-faced, if Chris hadn't pulled off two super saves to prevent Selworth adding to their 1–0 lead.

The only thing that cheered them up a little was the news coming through from the other game. Mark had taken charge of the phone.

'Don't worry, Dad says Ashford are losing too,' he announced. 'They kicked off before us and they're 2–1 behind in the second half.'

'Er . . . can we be sure your dad's right about the score?' Chris said hesitantly. 'I mean, you've often told us he gets numbers the wrong way round and stuff like that.'

'Surprised he even knows what number to dial,' added Rakesh. 'He's got a worse memory than you, Professor.'

Mark looked hurt, wishing his mum hadn't said anything about Dad forgetting to take the phone with him that morning. He'd driven halfway to Ashford before returning home to collect it.

'The phone does have a built-in memory system, y'know,' he sneered in reply. 'If you've ever used one.'

'Yeah, but has it got a calculator as well?'

As Mr Jones attempted to start his team talk, the phone rang and Mark clamped it to his ear. 'Hi, Dad . . . There's been another goal? Great! Is that 3–1 now? . . .'

Their hopes rose as they listened to Mark's end of the conversation.

'. . . Oh! You mean Ashford got it . . .'

Their faces fell.

'Sorry, guys,' Mark said with a shrug. 'Seems they've just gone and equalized. It's two–all there now.'

6 Wrong Numbers

As the teams lined up for the second half, Chris gazed around the crowded touchline. He had never seen so many Danebridge supporters at an away match before. But then, of course, this was no ordinary match. Their place in the league was at stake.

One particular person, however, was nowhere in sight and Chris was very glad about that. 'Bradshaw's face when everybody refused to bring him here this morning!' he chuckled to himself at the memory. 'Classic!'

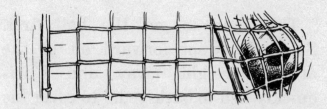

Chris had glanced out of the rear window as they drove off, just to check that Luke Bradshaw had been unsuccessful in cadging a lift. The outcast was standing alone on the pavement, snarling with fury at being left behind by the convoy of cars heading for Selworth.

'Get stuck in, Reds! Go for goals.'

Andrew's loud, clear voice carried across the pitch and snapped his younger brother's mind back into focus on the task in hand. Chris instantly forgot all about Luke Bradshaw.

'C'mon, team,' the captain yelled from the edge of his penalty area as Selworth kicked off. 'Big effort! Let's play them off the park.'

They had to get the ball first. Selworth swept forward on to the attack straight away and Chris quickly had to back-pedal to cover his goal.

'Mark up, defence,' he cried. 'Watch that number eight, Phil.'

Dinesh was the striker in question and he was proving a real handful for Philip, especially when the ball was on the ground. On this occasion, the winger sent over a high cross, which was far more to the centre-back's liking. He would give a giraffe a good contest in the air.

Philip's head met the ball firmly, clearing it well out of the penalty area to where Ryan was hovering. He linked up with Rakesh on the halfway line and a clever one-two sent Rakesh away, running deep into Selworth territory.

The winger had the speed and skill to take on two blue shirts and dribble past them before drilling the ball low into the goalmouth. Kerry's lightning strike was unstoppable. There was a flash of red and white at the near post and the ball was in the net.

'The equalizer!' cried Rakesh. 'Brilliant flick, Kez.'

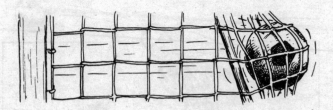

'One goal's not enough,' Kerry insisted, staying calm. 'We can't relax yet. We need another.'

Andrew grew more confident as he watched Danebridge take control and play their best football of the match. 'Just a matter of time before we score again,' he predicted. 'We're well on top now.'

Grandad shook his head. 'Don't count your chickens. A game's not over until the final whistle. You soon learn that in football, m'boy.'

The one at Ashford blew well in advance of Mr Carter's. The players soon became aware of that when they saw Mark jumping up and down in excitement, despite his bad leg. Mr

Jones had ordered him not to give out any more scores, but he just couldn't contain himself.

'The goals were really flying in at the end,' he shouted. 'Finished 4–3.'

'Who to?' demanded Rakesh. 'That's what we want to know.'

'Er . . . hold on, I can't quite make it out. The line's breaking up and I think Dad must be standing near a lot of people. They're all cheering . . .'

Andrew charged up to him. 'C'mon, who won, you nutter?' he screamed at Mark in frustration. 'Ashford or Highgate?'

'Er . . . not sure – Dad sounded a bit confused. Sorry.'

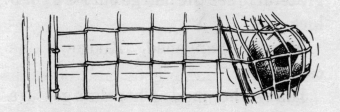

'Sorry! Is that all you can say?'

Mark shrugged and lowered the phone helplessly. 'Got cut off. Line's gone dead. The battery must be flat or something . . .'

His voice trailed away, half afraid that Andrew was going to hit him. The Danebridge team had virtually stopped playing, distracted by the drama on the touchline.

'Watch out!' shouted the headmaster. 'They're coming at us.'

His warning was almost too late. Philip stirred himself just in time to put in a challenge and make the attacker slice his shot against the post. Chris was nowhere near it and was grateful to see the ball go out for a goal-kick.

'What's happened, Andrew?' he called out.

His brother made a hopeless gesture

with his hands. 'Dunno. The mad professor and his dad have messed up. Best to assume Ashford have won. You've got to hang on for the draw now or you've had it.'

Rakesh ran up to the referee. 'How long to go, Mr Carter?'

The teacher glanced at his stop-watch. 'About five minutes yet.'

For the Danebridge players and supporters, those last few minutes were a slow, agonizing torture. They seemed more like five endless hours. One mistake now could send them down.

And there were lots of them. Panic set in and Selworth took advantage of their opponents' jitters. They pressed

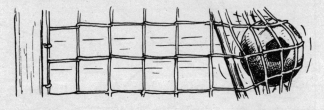

forward eagerly, sensing victory, and the Danebridge goal led a charmed life. Philip headed one effort off the line and another skimmed just wide of the upright.

When the ball fell to the feet of Dinesh inside the final minute of the game, however, the goal was at his mercy. Only Chris stood between the

striker and an inviting expanse of netting. The keeper flung himself recklessly into the line of fire and felt the shot slam into his body. He had no idea where the ball went to after that, apart from the fact that it didn't go past him.

Dinesh could hardly believe that he hadn't scored the winner. 'How did you stop that one?' he gasped.

'Luck mostly, I think,' Chris replied, shaking his head. 'I just had to get in the way of it.'

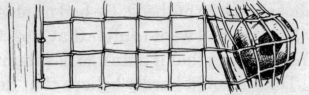

As applause echoed around the pitch for the magnificent save, the referee checked his watch again and the game moved into added time. There were only a few seconds left now for Danebridge to hold on.

Kerry gained possession of the ball near the right touchline and decided to run with it towards the corner flag in a bid to use up some valuable time. Two defenders tracked her down but with a shimmy and a wiggle, she was free and a path to goal suddenly opened up in front of her. It was too tempting to resist.

Two strange things happened then. The first was that Kerry opted to pass rather than shoot, a rare event in itself, and the second was that Rakesh headed the ball.

The shooting angle was too tight even for Kerry to think she could score and she whipped over a cross instead about waist height. Rakesh met it with a superb diving header at the far post, his body horizontal with the ground. He made contact with the ball a fraction before a defender's boot did so against his face.

The ball was in the net, the

Danebridge players were celebrating and the referee signalled the end of the match, but Rakesh was still lying flat out in the goalmouth. As his teammates helped the dazed scorer to sit up, they saw that his shirt was redder than anyone else's. Blood was dripping from his nose.

'Fantastic header, Rakky!' cried Ryan. 'We've won!'

'Have to get you cleaned up,' Kerry smiled. 'Looks like you've been in another fight with Luke.'

Rakesh managed a lopsided grin. 'Worth it. Feels even better to win this one – the fight against relegation!'

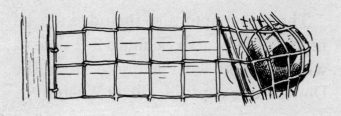

Monday's edition of the *Selworth Mail* printed a copy of the final league table, confirming Ashford's dramatic 4–3 victory that sent unlucky Brentway sinking into Division 2.

Bottom three places . . .

	P	W	D	L	F	A	Pts
					Goals		
Danebridge	16	4	4	8	24	33	16
Ashford	16	4	3	9	27	42	15
Brentway	16	3	5	8	20	38	14

The newspaper also included a brief report of Selworth School's 2–1 defeat, which ended with a quote from the Danebridge captain, Chris Weston:

'We just take each game as it comes. Now we're safe, we can't wait to play our next big match – the semi-final of the cup!'

THE END

ROB CHILDS
THE BIG
SEND-OFF

Illustrated by Jon Riley

YOUNG CORGI

Especially for Sam and Joe

1   Hit and Miss

'Pass it!'

It was the kind of demand that was very hard to refuse, but Rakesh had a good shooting chance himself and the goal looked so tempting. He drew his foot back, ready to pull the trigger – and then passed.

His teammate's shot snaked low towards the target. If the goalkeeper thought he had it covered, he was wrong. The ball skimmed wide of his

flailing hand, but thumped against the post and rebounded away.

'Bad luck, Kez,' cried Rakesh.

'Bad miss, more like. I should've scored. Why didn't *you* have a go?'

'You were screaming for a pass.'

'I wouldn't have passed to anybody else.'

'Now she tells me.'

Kerry pulled a face. 'You don't have to do everything I say, you know.'

'I don't,' he protested. 'It's just that . . .'

'Look, I'm fed up of you all trying to be nice to me just 'cos I'm leaving,' she said. 'It's only a football match. No big deal.'

The keeper interrupted them. 'Great effort, Kerry,' Chris praised her. 'Beat me all ends up for pace.'

She turned on the school team captain. 'And you're the worst one of the lot. Just shut up, will you!'

Kerry ran off to fetch the ball, leaving Chris Weston open-mouthed. 'What did I say to upset her?'

'Nothing,' grinned Rakesh. 'A bit of a touchy subject, that's all.'

'What is?'

'Missing it.'

'Everybody misses.'

'Yeah, but not the chance to play in a cup final,' Rakesh explained. 'She's trying not to show how much it means to her.'

'We're not even in the Final yet,' Chris pointed out. 'We've got to win the replay first.'

'You try telling Kez that. She wanted a medal, not compliments.'

The captain slipped Rakesh a sly wink as Kerry dribbled the ball back towards them. 'C'mon, then, bet you can't beat me from there,' he called out.

His playful taunt had the desired effect. Kerry flipped the ball up into the air and hit it sweetly on the volley. She only had a narrow shooting angle, but Chris was out of position and his dive was in vain. He might also have made the excuse of blurred vision.

The ball was travelling so fast that he barely saw it rocket past him.

'Not bad,' he grunted ruefully, picking himself up and trudging after the ball. There was no net to block its flight, but he didn't really mind the trek, pleased that the team's two main goalscorers seemed on song. It was just a pity that Kerry wouldn't be able to join in the final chorus with Rakesh.

'Still, one match at a time,' Chris sighed. 'That's what Grandad always says.'

Danebridge Primary School's last game before Easter was a cup semi-final replay at Great Norton. The delayed Final was now due to take place in the summer term – too late for Kerry. She would already be settling into her new school by then. Her parents had decided to expand their riding school business and they were moving to bigger premises elsewhere.

'Reckon we ought to try taking a few spot-kicks as well,' Rakesh suggested. 'The match might have to be decided on penalties in the end, remember.'

'Yeah, good idea,' Chris agreed. 'I

need some practice at trying to stop them too.'

'Sorry, guys, I've got to get off now,' said Kerry, collecting her bag from behind the goal. 'Promised Mum I'd help out in the stables before tea.'

It was rare for Kerry not to go straight home after school to be with all the horses. Staying behind on the village recreation ground for a while with some of her teammates was a sure sign of how determined she was to leave Danebridge on a high note.

'I'll take the first kick in any shootout,' said Rakesh, as Kerry trailed away. 'That'll get us off to a good start.'

'Not if it's anything like the last one you took in the league, it won't,' muttered Philip, their giant centre-back. 'The ball's still in orbit!'

Rakesh had rather hoped people

might have forgotten about that. 'Yeah, well, it hasn't put me off. I'm still confident of scoring.'

That was more than could be said for most of the others.

'Not as easy as it looks, is it?' grunted Philip as he watched his first wayward effort disappear into the distance.

When they'd each had two goes, only Rakesh and Ryan had enjoyed some success. Ryan was the youngest player in the squad, but he was already a proven goalscorer. Chris thought that was an important factor.

'When the pressure's really on, you need players who are used to scoring,' he said. 'That's why me and Philip are no good at penalties.'

They all tried again, but Rakesh missed this time as well. He sent Chris the wrong way, but put his kick wide of the target. The one triumph went to Paul, the left-back, who stroked the ball neatly inside the post.

'That's your theory shot down in flames, captain,' Paul laughed. 'I haven't scored a goal all season.'

Chris had no trouble saving the rest – or at least the ones he could reach. Many sailed harmlessly wide or high.

'What about Kez? Bet she'll be willing to take one,' said Rakesh. 'She'd just give their goalie a hard stare and he wouldn't dare save it!'

Chris smiled. 'Better not let her hear you say that. She'd lynch you from the crossbar.'

'Yeah, and then probably accuse me of being a goalhanger!'

Chris's grandad had been watching the footballers from the back garden wall of his cottage and now strolled over to have a word with them.

'Reckon I might put my pyjamas in the car tomorrow before we go to the match,' he chuckled.

'Pyjamas?' repeated Chris, puzzled.

'Well, if Great Norton are as bad as you lot at taking penalties, it could go on all night – the longest shootout in soccer history.'

2 On the Spot

'Easy! Easy!' Andrew chanted mockingly.

Chris glared up at his elder brother. 'Huh! Lucky, you mean. Went in off the post.'

'The perfect penalty,' Andrew claimed. 'No keeper could have got to that one, even if they'd dived the right way for it – which you didn't.'

Chris's teammates had all gone home by the time Andrew turned up on the recky to fetch his brother back for tea and found him having a personal coaching session with Grandad. The meal was forgotten.

'In my days as a keeper, y'know, we weren't allowed to move before the ball was kicked,' Grandad said. 'And I still believe it's best not to commit yourself too early. Just wait a split second till you see where the ball goes.'

'It might be too late then,' replied Chris.

'Aye, it might – if it's well struck. That last one would have been out of reach, anyway. But if the shot's a bit weak or not too wide of you, then you've got a chance of saving it.'

Chris crouched on his line to face the next penalty. He tried to put Andrew

off by whirling his arms about and then made a quick jerk to his right, as if he was going to dive in that direction. It seemed to make Andrew have a late change of mind and he scooped the ball to the keeper's left instead. Chris hurled himself after it, but he was nowhere near making contact. He would have needed elastic arms. The ball passed well wide of the post.

'Missed! Go and fetch it!' he laughed as Andrew slouched off after the ball. 'Sold you a brill dummy there.'

'Rubbish!' his brother denied hotly. He would never admit to being fooled. 'I meant to put it that side. Just a bit off target, that's all.'

Chris was still grinning as Andrew settled the ball on the spot again.

'You won't even smell this one, our kid. No more side-footed placing. This is gonna be a real mega-blaster.'

Chris wondered for a moment whether this was all a bluff, but knew it wasn't when Andrew straightened up. His face was red with frustration after that previous failure. The kicker meant business.

'Wait and see, remember, Chris,' Grandad called out as Andrew charged in. 'Stay on your feet as long as possible.'

Chris dodged about and flapped his arms to add to the distraction, but Andrew ignored such antics. He whacked the ball as hard as he could, vaguely to the right of the keeper, but Chris reacted well and deflected it up on to the underside of the crossbar.

The ball crashed against the woodwork and ricocheted to the ground before spinning away.

'Goal!' Andrew screamed. 'Bounced over the line.'

Chris had no idea where the ball landed. He sat in the goalmouth and looked at Grandad for the verdict.

'You must've seen it was in,' Andrew appealed desperately.

Grandad shook his head. 'Sorry, can't be sure from this angle. It happened too quickly for my old eyes to tell.'

'Huh! Goalkeepers' union, I bet,' snorted Andrew. 'Not fair. I demand to see a television replay.'

They all laughed, even Andrew. He knew he'd scored more than he'd missed. He'd been counting. And so had Chris.

'Wish I could make it to the match tomorrow,' Andrew said. 'I won't be able to get from school over to Great Norton in time to watch you.'

'Not to worry. You'll be able to see us win the Final instead after Easter. You can take a picture of me holding the Cup!'

'You'll be lucky. You haven't beaten Great Norton yet this season.'

'So? They haven't beaten us either. We've drawn every game. But there's got to be a winner in the end tomorrow, one way or the other.'

Andrew nodded. 'Right, then, our kid. We'd better give you a bit more practice or you're gonna be in real trouble if it comes down to penalties.'

'Um . . . by the looks of it, I'd say we might all be in a spot of bother now,' murmured Grandad, and the boys followed his line of sight.

His daughter – their mother – was striding purposefully across the footbridge over the River Dane. Somehow, they didn't think she had come to check on Chris's penalty-saving technique.

Danebridge's leading scorer gave his team a dream start to the replay.

As the ball floated into the crowded

185

goalmouth, Rakesh hung back on the edge of the penalty area, trying to create a bit of extra space for himself. It was a good decision. The ball was only half cleared and Rakesh pounced to lash it past the unsighted goal-keeper. It was the first time they'd actually had the lead against Great Norton in any of their previous meetings.

Not that they held it for long. Five minutes later, the ball was nestling in the back of the Danebridge net, put there by the home side's main danger man, Dan Robson. The winger had been too quick for Paul and too tricky for Chris, dribbling round the keeper before slotting the ball over the line.

The player who most caught the eye in the first half, however, was the visitors' slim, fair-haired number eight, the one with the bobbing ponytail.

Kerry Sharpe's goals had played a key part in the Danebridge cup run and she wanted to give her teammates a farewell present of at least one more.

The opposition remembered her well from the first semi-final. Kerry was proving a threat again every time she had the ball, and her rasping shot just before the interval brought out the very best in the Great Norton goal-keeper.

She struck the ball cleanly with her left foot but Wayne was well positioned, making sure there was no gap between his body and the near post. Even so, it was only due to his quick reflexes that he managed to tip the shot over the crossbar for a corner.

He grinned at the striker, but the look she gave him in return made his spine tingle. It was the smile on the face of the tiger – cold and deadly.

3 So Near, So Far

'Try and get tighter on that winger, Paul,' Chris said as the players sucked on their half-time slices of oranges. 'Don't give him too much space.'

Philip butted in. 'It needs somebody quicker to mark Dan.'

Paul scowled and tossed his chewed peel down onto the tray. 'Well, that rules you out, Daddy-Longlegs,' he retorted.

Chris knew the two defenders were not always the best of mates. 'Guess we might just have to put an extra man on him to cover you,' he said quickly before Philip could respond to Paul's jibe.

Mr Jones, their headmaster and coach, had come to the same conclusion. 'We'll play Mark a bit deeper this half and give Paul some back-up,' he declared, issuing instructions about the new tactics.

'Right pair together, them two, Paul and the Professor,' Philip sniggered. 'The only way they'll keep that Dan kid quiet is to bore him to death. Paul could hold him down while the Professor explains all about how to do fractions!'

Mark, the so-called Professor, was the school's star mathematician, but

his teammates had to be grateful if he remembered which way he was supposed to be kicking. At times, he still seemed to be working out problems in his head on the football field.

Much to Philip's surprise, Dan didn't enjoy a great deal of success against his twin markers. After the Professor had shaken him up with a crunching tackle early in the second half, Dan wasn't so keen to take him on again. He still had the beating of Paul, but preferred to pass the ball to someone else rather than risk another clash with the stocky number six.

It was left to Rakesh to demonstrate how to dribble past two defenders. His footwork was dazzling. Collecting the ball near the right touchline, he slipped it through the legs of the first then bamboozled the next with a late body swerve and change of pace.

Rakesh ran free up the wing, having time to pick out Kerry as the target for his low cross, but he was lucky to find her with it. The ball clipped somebody's knee and the deflection looped over Wayne's head to drop kindly on to Kerry's behind him. She wasn't able to get much power on the header, but it was enough to guide the ball just inside the post into the net.

'Good job you were only a couple of metres out,' laughed Rakesh as they celebrated. 'Any further and it would never have reached.'

'Concentrate, team,' yelled Chris from his goal. 'Just hold on for a few more minutes and we're in the Final.'

There was longer to go than Chris hoped. Their 2–1 advantage was made to look very slender as the Danebridge team suffered a collective attack of the jitters. Mistakes occurred all over the pitch – miskicks, misplaced passes, mistimed challenges and missed chances.

But when the equalizer did come, it was because of a double piece of misfortune. Philip slipped over as he tried to cut out a centre, causing Paul and Mark to collide with each other in their panic to clear the ball. Dan did well not to collapse with laughter at such a pantomime of errors and stayed on his feet long enough to steer his shot past the helpless Chris.

A short while later, the referee gave a loud blast on his whistle. 'Extra time now, teams,' he announced. 'Five minutes each way.'

'We seem fated to draw with Great Norton this season,' sighed Mr Jones. 'Might have guessed this would happen.'

Grandad was standing next to the headmaster. 'Aye, and you know what I'm thinking,' he murmured. 'Penalties, here we come.'

Extra time was a nervous, scrappy affair, with defences well on top. Neither side wanted to commit too many people to the attack in case they were caught on the break. Goalscoring chances were few and far between. Any bad mistake now and they knew their team would be out of the Cup.

Chris and Wayne were almost unemployed – apart from one heart-

stopping moment for Great Norton when Kerry flashed a shot into the side netting. But the two keepers were about to become very busy people indeed.

'*Peeeeeepppppp!*' went the final whistle.

'All right, everyone,' said the neutral referee. 'Scores level at two goals each. Penalty shootout.'

The Danebridge players looked towards the headmaster. He had not said anything to them about which three he wanted to take the kicks – mainly because he hadn't yet decided himself.

'Um . . .' he faltered. 'Any volunteers . . . ?'

All the practice in the world would not have enabled Chris to save the opening penalty. His reaction was good, throwing himself forward to his left, but the placement of the kick was even better. The ball smacked high into the net, well out of the goal-keeper's reach.

'Good luck, Rakky!' Chris shouted, as he went to stand and wait outside the area while Wayne took his turn in goal.

By contrast, Rakesh aimed low for

the bottom corner, but didn't strike the ball as cleanly as he might have done. There was a flash of yellow across the goal and the ball was parried away. Wayne stood up triumphantly, the cheers of the home supporters ringing in his ears.

As Dan trotted forward to take Great Norton's second penalty, Rakesh slumped to the ground in the centre-circle, hardly daring to watch what happened. Kerry tapped him gently on the shoulder, but he didn't look up. He didn't want to listen to anybody's attempts at consolation.

Dan and Chris caught each other's eye for a moment, accepting the challenge of the duel. On the referee's whistle, Dan began his curving approach and Chris guessed from the angle of the run-up which side it might go – and the guess was a good one. He

dived to his right at full stretch and blocked the ball, knocking it firmly aside.

Dan could not believe it. It was the first penalty he had ever missed. Now he knew how wretched Rakesh was feeling.

Only four of the Reds had raised their hand in response to the head-master's appeal. One of them was Paul. He now placed the ball on the spot, took several paces back and waited for the referee's signal, breathing deeply to try and remain calm. He then loped in and sent Wayne the wrong way as he stroked the ball with his left foot towards the opposite corner.

CLUNK!

The ball struck the inside of the post and rebounded harmlessly across the goal in front of the relieved keeper.

Danebridge's hopes sank.

'Still one–nil to Great Norton,' called out the referee. 'Last goes coming up.'

4   Do or Die

'*Stay on your feet – don't dive too soon.*'

Grandad's words nudged their way into Chris's mind as he bounced up and down on the goal-line to relieve his tension. The Great Norton captain had taken responsibility for their final kick, hoping to clinch victory for his team. If he scored, it would be the end of the contest.

'*Stay on your feet . . .*'

Chris was very glad that he heeded the advice. The kick was hard and true, and hurtled straight at his head. Almost in self-defence, he blocked the ball with his arms and it spiralled up into the air over the crossbar.

'Still one–nil,' the referee called out. 'Third and last go for Danebridge.'

If Ryan was nervous, he didn't show it. When the ball was tossed his way, he casually flicked it up into his hands and plonked it on the penalty spot.

'Ready, lad?' asked the referee, seeing that the boy had only taken a couple of short steps back.

Ryan nodded. This was all the run-up he'd found he needed during the recky practice. As soon as the whistle sounded, Ryan moved in and chipped the ball cheekily over Wayne's diving body. Had Wayne stayed on *his* feet, he would have saved it easily.

The cup-tie was still alive – but not for very much longer.

'Scores tied, so now it's sudden death,' the referee announced. 'One penalty for each team until one scores and the other misses.'

Chris was taken aback when he saw who was facing him for this crucial penalty – Wayne.

'Somebody's got to do it,' he said with a sheepish shrug of the shoulders. 'And no-one else wanted the job.'

Wayne decided to rely on power and treated it like a goal-kick. He didn't have enough confidence in his own ability to make the ball go exactly where he aimed. As Chris dived, he knew he was beaten for pace – but the ball screamed over the bar and was last seen disappearing among the vehicles in the school car park.

'Wish I hadn't bothered now,' Wayne sighed miserably.

'At least you were brave enough to try,' said Chris, feeling a measure of sympathy for his opposite number.

Chris wondered if his own turn would come. As captain, he felt obliged to volunteer his services, if necessary – but he was relieved not to have to do that just yet. There was still at least one player who was keen to have a go.

'OK, Kerry, just give it your best shot,' said Mr Jones, admiring the girl's nerve. 'Show the lads how to do it.'

Kerry had never had the opportunity to take a penalty in a proper match, but she couldn't see what the problem was. The whole goal yawned in front of her and only the keeper stood in her way. And she simply pretended he wasn't there. It felt almost as if she was in a world of her own. She wasn't even aware of some unsporting whistles from a section of the home crowd.

'My last kick for Danebridge,' she murmured. 'Better make it count.'

And she did. Wayne got his hand close to it, but not close enough. The accuracy of the kick into the bottom left-hand corner of the net was too much for him.

Chris ran up to Kerry to give her a

special hug of delight. 'Great stuff, Kez!' he cried. 'Knew you'd do it for us.'

Kerry looked rather alarmed. For an awful moment, she thought that Chris had been going to kiss her!

'Up to you lot now so don't go and mess things up,' she said after the rest of the Danebridge squad had mobbed their heroine too. 'Just make sure you win that Cup.'

Grandad turned to the beaming headmaster. 'It's going to be quite a test for the lads to play the Final without that lass in the team.'

'Maybe – but the main thing is that they now have a chance to pass it,' Mr Jones replied. 'And I'm one of those teachers who believe that tests often bring out the best in people.'

The footballers pooled their pocket money and bought Kerry a leaving present on the final day of term – a leather football.

'Er, didn't think it was worth trying to wrap it,' Chris said bashfully as he handed the ball over at morning play-time. 'It's just something to remember us by.'

'Yeah, and make good use of it, too,' added Rakesh. 'We don't want to have wasted our money. Keep on playing the game at your next school – you're a star!'

Kerry grinned to cover her embarrassment. 'Don't worry, I won't be hanging my boots up yet. Might even bring my new teammates back to Danebridge next season and thrash you!'

'Huh!' snorted Philip. 'In your dreams!'

'I don't dream about football,' she smiled. 'Only horses.'

The following morning, a kickabout on the recky was interrupted by the arrival of a familiar figure on horseback.

'Want a game?' asked Chris.

'Hey! This isn't polo, you know,' Paul cut in, grinning.

'No, it's OK, thanks, not today,' Kerry replied. 'Just letting little Jonesy have a last look round the village.'

She gave her palomino pony a pat as the players laughed. Chris was the only one who'd known that Kerry had named it after their headmaster.

'You will come and watch us in the Final, won't you, like you promised?' he said. 'You know the date.'

211

'I promised I'd try,' she reminded him. 'It's too far to ride, so I'll have to hope Mum or Dad can spare the time to drive me over.'

'You'll have to be a good girl and muck out the stables every day during the holidays,' grinned Rakesh.

'I do that anyway. I love it,' she laughed. 'But are you guys really worth getting my hands dirty for, I wonder?'

'You come and watch and we'll prove it,' Chris retorted.

It was brave talk. Their big test in the Final could not come any bigger. It was against their arch-rivals, Shenby – a team that had already done the double over Danebridge in the League. There was no doubt as to which school were the Cup favourites.

5   *Final Challenge*

'Doesn't seem the same without Kez around, does it?' observed Rakesh.

'We could ask Ryan to do his hair in a ponytail, if you like,' Philip said with a grin. 'See if that might help.'

Rakesh wasn't amused. 'Huh! It's not so bad for you. I've lost my strike partner.'

'It's bad for all of us. Her goals have been crucial since she came into the team after Christmas.'

The football season had now

stretched into the summer term and the squad was practising for the Cup Final. It would be their last game together. The boys knew that if the Final itself were drawn, there was no provision for a replay, nor even any extra time or penalties. The trophy would simply be shared between the two schools – just as in the previous season when the Weston brothers had helped to inspire a Danebridge fight-back.

Chris hurled the ball away to send his team on to the attack in their six-a-side game, but the Professor dithered in possession and Mr Jones halted play. 'Let the ball do the work, Mark,' he said. 'Pass it more quickly.'

The Professor wasn't the only one who appeared sluggish. Mr Jones was more than a little concerned about the attitude of several players. 'Come on,

lads, wake up,' he urged. 'Looks like some of you think you're still on holiday. You'll have to be much sharper against Shenby or they'll walk all over you.'

They perked up a bit after that but their overall performance did not fill the headmaster with optimism. He decided to squeeze in an extra practice session before the Final. It looked as though they were going to need it.

Chris confided his own doubts about their Cup chances to Andrew that evening, but he didn't receive much sympathy.

'You're not a one-girl team, y'know,' Andrew scoffed. 'You can't rely on Kerry riding up on her white charger to rescue you.'

'I know that. It's just that Rakesh and Ryan don't have the same kind of understanding yet up front.'

'Shenby will stuff you, anyway – with or without Kerry,' Andrew smirked. 'They've done so twice already in the League.'

'So? Like Grandad says, every game's different.'

'If that's the case, how come you kept on drawing with Great Norton?'

Chris frowned. 'I'm just saying it's a pity Kerry won't be able to play, that's all. She really wanted that medal.'

'She could still have one.'

'How do you mean?'

'Well, there's probably still time for old Jonesy to arrange for an extra medal to be presented to her after the match.'

Chris's face lit up. 'Why didn't I think of that? I'll ask him tomorrow. That'd be a sure-fire way of getting her there somehow – even on a white charger!'

Chris's mind was racing ahead. Another idea was taking shape now, but he decided to keep it to himself – just in case things didn't work out as he hoped on Saturday.

There were no horses of any description to be seen as the Cup Final kicked off. And no Kerry either. Mr Jones had agreed about the special medal and notified her parents, but there was still no guarantee that she would be able to attend. Everyone was hard at work at the new stables.

'C'mon, the Reds!' cried Andrew as Danebridge's red-striped shirts launched their first attack against the Blues of Shenby. 'Let's have a goal.'

For all his teasing of his younger brother, Andrew was keen that his old school should retain the trophy. The match was being played on his new 'home' ground, the playing fields of Selworth Comprehensive, and he knew the big pitch well. He'd already warned Chris that the goalmouths were bare and bumpy after a season's hard use.

Grandad was standing next to Andrew on the touchline and groaned inwardly as Rakesh overran the ball and lost possession. 'If the lads are not on top form today, I fear our Chris could be in for a busy time,' he said.

Andrew nodded. 'Right, some of my mates here at the Comp are ex-Blues. They reckon Shenby's side this year is better than their own – only got pipped for the League on goal difference and the players want to make up for that now by winning the Cup.'

Chris had no time to dwell on Kerry's non-appearance. He was already busy enough, trying to keep the lively Shenby attack at bay. Twice the ball thudded reassuringly into his green jersey and he also leapt high to pluck a dangerous cross out of the air. His safe handling was a confidence booster to all his defence.

Unfortunately, this didn't seem to spread as far as the forward line. The Reds' own attacks tended to fizzle out before they had a clear sight of the Shenby goal. Their only shot of the game thus far had come from a long-range punt by the Professor that veered away to hit a post – the one holding the corner flag.

It came as little surprise to any of the large crowd of spectators when Shenby took a deserved lead. The move started with a neat exchange of passes up the left wing and was ended by a lethal strike from just inside the penalty area. It was a goal fit to grace a Cup Final, applauded by Danebridge and Shenby supporters alike.

Chris was clapping, too, but not in appreciation of the goal. He was encouraging his teammates to keep battling away. 'C'mon, let's get the ball in their half of the pitch for a change,'

he called out. 'Rakky's hardly had a kick yet.'

'Reckon that's what they all need to get them going this morning,' Grandad muttered to himself. 'A good kick up the backside!'

Two things happened just before the break that altered the course of the game. The first was that Danebridge equalized.

The goal was totally against the run of play, but it served to show that no team can afford to relax, even when they are well on top. Ryan swept in from the left flank, stumbled through a half-hearted challenge and managed to work the ball on to his right foot.

'Kez would've shot from here,' he thought. 'So will I.'

The Blues' defence had backed off, expecting Ryan to pass, but they let him advance too far. He made them

pay for such casualness, although his shot would not have been in the same class as Shenby's as a candidate for any *Goal of the Season* competition.

Ryan didn't strike the ball cleanly and it also took a slight deflection off a defender's leg. The goalkeeper still appeared to have the shot well covered, but he was unlucky – and perhaps rather lazy too. The ball hit a rut just in front of him and kept low, evading his grasp. Sadly for Shenby, he had failed to ensure that he had some part of his body in line with the shot. There was nothing behind his hands to stop the ball apart from the net.

The second event was an even bigger

shock than the equalizing goal. The Professor was sent off!

'Off! Off! Off!'

A small group of former Shenby pupils started up the chant for a laugh after the Blues' number ten had been clumsily brought down outside the penalty area. It wasn't the first foul that Mark had committed in the game – nor was it the worst – but his accompanying cheek ensured that it was his last.

'I've already warned you about late tackles,' said the referee, taking out his notebook. 'What's your name?'

'The Professor,' Mark answered flippantly, not realizing the seriousness of the situation.

'Don't mess me about, lad. The foul was bad enough. The player was through on goal and certain to score.'

That remark offended Mark's sense

of mathematical probability. 'You can't say that,' he replied. 'He was coming in at about forty-five degrees and the keeper was making the shooting angle even more acute . . .'

Mark might have gone on to take speed and distance travelled into account, not to mention ground conditions, before arriving at an estimated ratio of the boy's chances of finding the net – say, one in four – but he wasn't given the opportunity. He received his marching orders instead.

It was so rare for players of this age

to be sent off that everyone was stunned by the dismissal, including Mark. He trailed off the pitch, shaking his head in disbelief that the referee hadn't agreed with such a logical analysis.

His teammates were punished twice over. Not only were they now a player short, but they also went 2–1 behind. They hastily built a ramshackle, red-striped wall to try and withstand the expected blast of the free-kick, but were then caught out by a cleverly flighted chip. The number ten exacted full revenge for his trip, rising unmarked at the far post to head Shenby back into the lead.

'We've had it now,' groaned Chris, fishing the ball out of the net in disgust. 'Sorry, Kez, we're letting you down.'

6 Ten Men

'Hey! Kez's here at last!' whooped Ryan. 'She'll bring us good luck.'

'Better do, 'cos we sure need some,' said Paul as the players gathered around Mr Jones for a half-time pep talk. The sight of Kerry climbing out of her father's car cheered them all up far more than any words the headmaster could find to say in the circumstances.

He tried a different tactic instead. 'I hope Kerry hasn't had a wasted journey,' he began. 'I wasn't going to tell you this, but I'm afraid the only extra medal available was a winners' one. They didn't have any spare losers'.'

'Sorry I'm late, guys,' Kerry apologized as she joined the group.

'Got your boots with you?' asked Philip to break the embarrassed silence. 'We might need you to come on as sub.'

'Riding boots, yeah – they're in the car,' she laughed. 'I've just come to see how you lot are coping without me. Have I missed much?'

'Not as much as you do when you're playing,' Rakesh grinned.

'Well, there is one thing you've missed, actually.'

Kerry turned round to see where the voice had come from. The Professor was sitting on the grass nearby,

wearing his tracksuit top. 'We wanted
to give you a good send-off, but I guess
I've already gone and done that!' he
admitted, managing a lopsided smile.

Mark's unexpected joke at his own
expense helped further to lift the mood
of gloom and doom that had been
hanging over everybody until Kerry's
timely arrival.

'Not to worry, Professor – we forgive
you for once,' said Rakesh. 'We'll just
have to prove to you now that ten can
sometimes be greater than eleven.'

'What's been happening?' Kerry demanded, puzzled. 'Aren't you winning?'

'Er, not exactly,' said Chris, glancing around at his teammates. 'But we're going to now – right?'

'Right!' they responded with renewed determination.

'C'mon, let's win this for Kez!' Rakesh cried as the ten-man team took the field again for the second half. 'We can still do it.'

Rakesh showed the way by example. Just a couple of minutes after the restart, his pace allowed him to explode past two defenders to reach a cross from Paul. It would have been a goal to rival Shenby's for quality, but

Rakesh's first-time strike flew narrowly wide of the target.

'Making it look as if we're the ones with the extra player, not Shenby,' said Grandad as Danebridge strung together a series of fine moves. 'What on earth did you say at half-time to fire them up?'

Mr Jones chuckled. 'I just applied a bit of amateur psychology.'

'How do you mean?'

'They think Kerry won't get a medal unless they win. I just hope they don't find out later that the medals are the same for both teams!'

The goalmouth nearer the school was seeing most of the action again, but now it was the Shenby keeper who found himself under siege. He was anxious to make up for his earlier error over the goal and did so with two brilliant saves to thwart Rakesh and Ryan, besides blocking Philip's powerful header from a corner.

Suddenly, Shenby broke free of the shackles and stormed forward up the right wing, catching Danebridge at full stretch. Paul and Philip were the only defenders back in position and they were heavily outnumbered, four against two.

The winger beat Paul for speed and although Philip got his head to the cross, the ball fell to the feet of the number ten on the left of the area. Chris had to scuttle across his goal to face the new threat as the boy struggled to control the ball on the bumpy ground. Even so, the goal-keeper had precious little time to react and his save was based on pure instinct. He threw up an arm and tipped the rising shot just over the crossbar.

If Shenby had gone two goals ahead at that point, the mountain might have been too steep for Danebridge to climb. As it was, the Reds took heart from their escape and, five minutes later, they forced a second equalizer.

Ryan beat his marker to the ball and looked up with a view to trying his luck again. Give Kerry the slightest glimpse of the goal and she would always shoot, but Rakesh's call this

time did not fall on deaf ears. Shaping as if to shoot, Ryan slipped the ball through to Rakesh on his right with a lovely disguised pass. Danebridge's leading scorer did the rest, drilling his shot into the corner of the net under the goalie's despairing dive.

The Shenby players had enjoyed too many comfortable victories over the course of the season and were not prepared for such a fight. They'd assumed they only had to turn up today to win, but they were about to be proved wrong.

With their normally solid defence now in disarray, the Blues' main hope seemed to be one of survival until the final whistle. Their time-wasting tactics and panicky clearances brought them no respite. The ball kept coming straight back into their own penalty area – and eventually into their own net again.

Rakesh carved open a gap for himself with a burst of acceleration up the right touchline and he screwed the ball across the face of the goal. It eluded the lunges of several players, including the keeper, and looked to be passing out of harm's way until a long leg stretched out to make contact.

And ten-year-old legs did not come any longer than Philip's. Sliding in at the far post, feet first, the gangling centre-back's left boot got the vital touch and knocked the ball over the line into the net.

Danebridge's celebrations knew no bounds. Chris ran the length of the pitch to throw himself on top of the pile of bodies that buried the scorer, and Kerry was sorely tempted to run on to the pitch and do the same.

'Well, well, who would have believed it?' murmured Grandad when the match ended shortly afterwards. 'Beaten Shenby 3–2 with only ten men!'

'That's what the Cup's all about,' Andrew grinned. 'Giantkilling.'

Chris led his victorious players towards the table where the medal presentations were soon to be made, signalling for the Professor and Kerry to join them. Andrew greeted his brother on the way with a great bear hug.

'You lucky thing, our kid!' he cried. 'Now you're gonna do something I'd have loved to – lift that Cup into the air.'

'Think I might be able to use some help,' Chris smiled.

In his excitement, Andrew jumped to the wrong conclusion. 'I can't go up with you,' he said, although he wouldn't have taken much persuading.

'I wasn't thinking of you,' Chris laughed. 'I want somebody else to share the honour with me.'

So when the winning captain was called upon to receive the silver trophy, Kerry was caught by surprise. Chris pushed her forward ahead of him into the clearing around the table. She resisted at first, not knowing what was happening, but in front of so many people, she wasn't in a position to argue.

Shyly, but proudly, Chris and Kerry held up the Cup between them for all the clicking cameras. Now she would not only have a medal to remind her of Danebridge's triumph, but also her picture in the local paper with the Cup.

Kerry had won many prizes and rosettes at gymkhanas but, just at this magic moment, this football trophy was even more special to her. She'd been part of a team and it felt good — very good indeed.

THE END

ABOUT THE AUTHOR

Rob Childs was born and grew up in Derby.
His childhood ambition was to become an
England cricketer or footballer – preferably
both! After university, however, he went into
teaching and taught in primary and high
schools in Leicestershire, where he now lives.
Always interested in school sports, he coached
school teams and clubs across a range of
sports, and ran area representative teams in
football, cricket and athletics.

Recognizing a need for sports fiction for young
readers, he decided to have a go at writing
such stories himself and now has more than
seventy books to his name, including the
popular *The Big Match* series, published by
Young Corgi Books.

Rob has now left teaching in order to be able to
write full-time. Married to Joy, a writer herself,
Rob is also a keen photographer, providing
many pictures for Joy's books and articles.